Picking Up Pieces

Thomas Shea, Volume 1

Griffith D Pritchard

Published by Griffith D Pritchard, 2022.

PICKING UP PIECES

First edition. January 21, 2022.

ISBN: 979-8201601430

Written by Griffith D Pritchard.

To my dear Aunt Florence, your memories and teachings have stayed with me. Thank you.

Picking Up Pieces

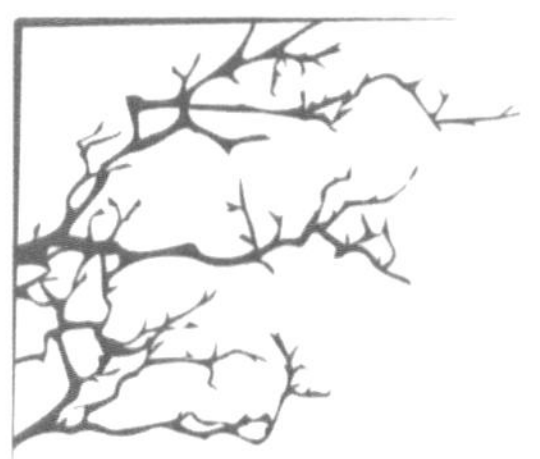

Chapter 1

Brian sits in an old dark blue Subaru Outback near the shoreline of Lake Erie as wind from a December snowstorm rocks the vehicle back and forth. He stares into the rear-view mirror trying to decide what he's going to do next. The dashboard lights softly brightens his face as an evil fire burns hotter and hotter in his hazel eyes. He keeps staring as he wonders if he really wants to go through with this. Does he really want to turn the clock back to the life he once lived doing whatever he had to do to survive?

Then he remembers why he's here. His eyes narrow as memories return. No, turning back isn't an option, not after what happened. He shifts the Outback into drive and heads down a snowy gravel road. As he gets closer to the lapping waters hitting icy shorelines, a massive concrete grain elevator rises up through the darkness and windswept snow. Brian parks in front of dilapidated double-wooden doors leading into the elevator and exits his car.

Stepping up to the doors, he sets down a brown gym bag in the snow. He pulls a key out of the left side pocket of his long black wool coat and slips it into a lock holding a chain together around the handles of the doors.

He removes the chain, picks up the bag, and steps inside.

The inside of the abandoned concrete grain elevator is as cold as the outside. Large funnels hang from the ceiling. They were once used to pour grain taken from the bowels of large ships roaming the waters of the Great Lakes and into rail cars that rested on the tracks sitting underneath them. From there, the grain was moved to factories throughout the Northeast to make cereals, breads, cosmetics, fuels, and more. But now, the concrete ceiling and walls around the funnels are decayed and crumbling, and ships no longer dock outside the building for offloading.

His footsteps echo in the desolation as he makes his way into an abandoned office with a portable kerosene heater humming in the stillness.

In the darkness, the sound of someone tugging on a pull cord rings out. Almost immediately, a gas-powered generator starts, and a portable work light powers up. In the middle of the room, the growing light shines on an exhausted-looking man with his hands, feet, and chest bound to a metal desk chair with duct tape.

The tied man looks up at him.

"Why, Brian?" he asks.

Brian looks down at him; there's an angry determination in his eyes.

"I want you to know this hasn't been easy for me," Brian responds as he lets out a deep sigh. "I've spent countless hours praying I'd get over it, but I can't."

Fear in the bound man's face grows.

"What are you going to do?" he asks.

Brian ignores him. "Why didn't you listen to me? I told you about Gretchen. I saw it in her eyes."

"We can't go by that," the man says.

"You don't know what I know about people. You should have listened. Everyone has an aura. Hers was the devil's, and yours was being an arrogant prick who thought he learned it all in the books he read. You really don't learn much from the books you read, you know? You can't. Not this type of shit. Not the shit I know."

"Brian, there was nothing we could do."

"Didn't you see what I was telling you?" pain wells up in Brian's eyes. "Didn't you?"

"Brian, it's not that simple," The man's voice trails off. "She hadn't done anything."

"Yes, it is. It's very simple. You eliminate the threat before it gets you. How can you people not see that?"

"We can't...Brian, I realize...I realize I could have done better. I think about it every day."

"Damn right, you could have done a lot better. You and the others."

"Others? What others?"

Brian walks around to the back of the chair, opens the brown gym bag, and pulls out a polyurethane body suit, gloves, and skull cap.

"Shelly, for one."

A surge of energy overcomes the man as he struggles against the ropes to free himself as Brian zips up the suit.

"You leave my wife out of this! She wasn't in control of anything."

A chilliness enters Brian's voice. "She's not your wife anymore."

"Just the same. Shelly had absolutely no control over what happened. She didn't even really work there."

"Everyone had more control than Jennifer, and none of you listened, including Shelly."

Brian removes a sharp-bladed hunting knife out of a sheath he carries on his belt and steps up directly behind the man.

"I'm going to see her, you know," Brian says.

"Why?"

"Because I plan on seeing everyone. I would tell you how it goes, but there's going to be a problem."

"What's that?"

Brian grabs the man's hair on his forehead and pulls his head back as far as he can. He slices open the man's neck from ear to ear and beyond.

"You won't be here," Brian says menacingly as the man's blood spurts everywhere while his heart continues to pump blood. Blood that gets all over the floor and on Brian's polyurethane suit.

With a couple of extra heavy slices, the man's head disconnects from his body.

Blood pulsates from the throat area of the headless body as Brian drags it by its feet across the dusty and dirty rail tracks running under the large funnels hanging from the ceiling. The blood leaves a dark red trail from the back room to the front doors of the grain elevator.

He drags the body until he gets it to his car parked outside the front doors of the massive grain elevator. He raises the hatch of the Subaru and lifts the body up onto a plastic sheet covering the inside of the trunk.

Then he goes back inside and gets the head.

Driving over to Gallagher's Beach, directly next to the grain elevator, he parks near the base of a wooden pier jutting out past the frozen shoreline to open water. As he gets out of his car, he looks at the lights shining over at the Small Boat Harbor Marina parking lot a few hundred yards away. The light stops before it reaches him, and he feels sure no one can see him as he removes the head and body from the car. He places the head on the body's chest and starts pulling it over the mounting snow to the end of the pier.

The heaviness of the limp body makes it hard to move through the thickening snow, and it takes several minutes before he gets to the end of the pier. Brian grabs the body under the armpits and hoists it halfway over the railing. Then he reaches down and flips the legs over. The body hits a post as it drops into the water.

Brian quickly looks around to make sure no one is close enough to hear after the body makes a bigger splash sound than he expected.

Feeling safe, he grabs the head by its hair and swings it around with his arm, and launches it into the water as far as he can throw.

Brian watches for a few moments as the head and body flow away toward the Niagara River, where he hopes they will eventually make their way over the falls and into the whirlpool below. A whirlpool known to suck bodies into its vortex to keep them forever pressed to the river's floor.

As he watches the body parts float into the night's darkness, the realization that he's now reached the point of no return sinks in. He knows life will never be the same.

The thought sends shivers down his spine.

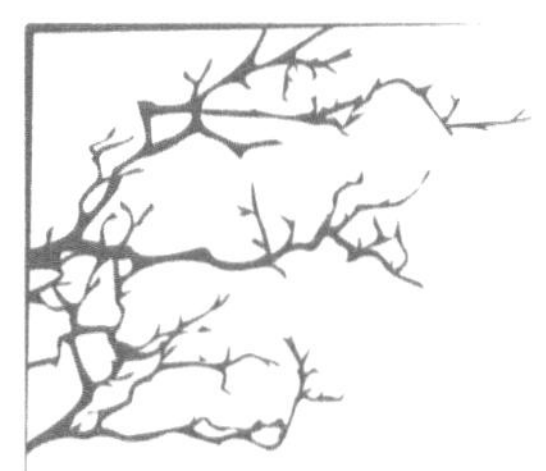

Chapter 2

Brian emerges from the darkness as he walks into the yellowish light coming from old-time globed street lamps planted in front of St. Joseph's Old Cathedral in downtown Buffalo. He looks up at the tall oak doors at the top of stone steps and reflects back to when he first walked up them to enter the single-steepled Gothic-Revival building built with gray stones. Stones that were harvested from a pit near the Erie Canal locks in Lockport, New York in the late-1800s.

Back then, Brian was looking for a new path in life where he could do good and forget about who he was and from where he came. He was one of the unwashed who roamed streets at night in search of food and shelter while passing empty storefronts filled with addicts and perverts hiding in the dark doorways seeking their pleasure, and where suburban men came in their fancy cars to offer young boys and girls a few dollars for a couple of moments of their time. Sometimes, he'd give in because the momentary warmth of a man who disgusted him was better than sitting in the cold and rain during the night. Besides, money always came in handy when hunger burned in his belly.

Giving in created an anger that burned in his soul. An anger that led him to carry a switchblade knife and use it when it was necessary. How many times he used it didn't matter once he stopped looking at the faces of the men who stared down at him while they pushed his head harder down into their laps before pulling it back up again by his hair.

Then one day, he couldn't take it anymore. He was wasting his life, and he knew it. The search for change led him to the tall oak doors and Father Isaiah.

Father Isaiah was a blessed person who roamed the streets at night in search of lost souls he could help. Brian knew of him by talking to those who huddled underneath the abutments of city bridges to escape the snow and wind. He was a legend among those who felt he had come to this earth to help them.

Brian hoped he would help him, too. He remembers the fear he felt as he first walked up the stone steps. The fear gave him a funny feeling - like he was afraid he might get rejected, and getting rejected just wasn't something he would worry about. Hell, that never happened!

But walking up these steps, he was looking for a new life. A better life. One where he might eventually be able to help others who walk down the dark paths he's always known. Now, he was scared; what if he told the truth and Father Isaiah threw him out?

Or, worse yet, what if he tells him about what he's done, and the father, in turn, wants him to do some of those things for him? What if this saint of the streets is just another fake living a lie? It wouldn't be the first time he experienced that.

He didn't know what to expect. All he knew was that he was tired and lost, and he desperately wanted to feel better about himself. Life has risks. He knows this. And the hope of something better was stronger than staying where he was.

So, he finished walking up the steps and into the warm and welcoming arms of Father Isaiah. A man who gave without any care of getting something in return. He was real, and he was vibrant. His dark brown eyes gleamed from his cherub brown face as he spoke of how Brian could come and stay to help out. And, if there's one thing Father Isaiah needed , it was help running the grand cathedral.

Brian got into a brothership program and became like the young brother Father Isaiah lost during the Iraqi War. The good father entrusted him with responsibilities Brian never dreamed of having. He remembers how Father Isaiah gave him the money from the collections and asked him to take it to a nearby bank for deposit. The feeling Brian had as he proudly walked to the bank with thousands of dollars in his hand was indescribable. He thought about how he now had enough money to run away and hide, but he told himself "no" and walked into the bank.

Father Isaiah providing moments like these changed his life. He thought it had changed his life forever.

Now, he's starting to feel like it was all a waste. That he shouldn't have even tried. He should have known better he thinks as he kicks himself with his mind. Why would a loser like me ever end up doing good? There's a reason they threw me away, he ponders. *They* were those who brought him into this world only to leave him abandoned while *they* satisfied their own needs in whatever way *they* could. *They* also set him out on his own before he was old enough to get a real job, even if it paid pennies. Instead, as a young child, he was forced out onto the streets and left to survive on his own in whatever way he could.

Now, Brian walks up the steps of the imposing structure once again, but this time without the feeling of hope in his soul. He swiftly walks down the right aisle of the cavernous interior toward a statue of the Virgin Mary and a table full of candles, some lit, some not, underneath it.

The soles of his oxford shoes make a unique clicking sound as he walks over the terrazzo tiles on the floor. When he reaches the statue, Brian pulls a bill out of his pocket and places it into a slot on a box on the table of candles. He grabs a long wooden match, lights it, and, with shaking hands, struggles to put the flame to the wick of one of the candles. As the flame lights the wick, Brian gets down on his knees, bows his head, and closes his eyes.

His body starts to shake as he begins to sob. The shaking becomes uncontrollable as the reality of what he has done tonight continues to sink in. He feels like the blood in his head is boiling and ready to explode.

He gets up and races across the altar into the vestry, where the priests hang their robes and store the wine. He goes through a door into the hallway leading to the rectory where he lives with Father Isaiah.

Father Isaiah steps out of the library room as Brian hurriedly stampers down the hallway toward the bedrooms. The sight immediately causes him to be concerned.

"Brian," Father Isaiah calls out to him softly in the quietness of the night.

Brian pays no attention to him and keeps on racing down the hallway to his bedroom. He steps inside and shuts the door.

Father Isaiah steps up to the door moments later and gently taps on it with the knuckle of his middle finger.

Panic fills Brian's eyes as he looks at the door. He hadn't noticed anyone in the hallway and was surprised by the tap. He hears another couple of taps, and he forces himself to stay very still.

Out in the hallway, Father Isaiah's concern grows, but he feels now might not be the time to address the issue. He walks to his bedroom and wonders about what is going on. It leaves him uneasy.

Brian begins to breathe again when he hears Father Isaiah walk away. The room seems to be spinning as he climbs into his bed and gets under the covers without bothering to undress. He stares through the darkness at the ceiling, thinking about the hole he once climbed out. A hole he now feels he's about to fall back into - correction, a hole he *has* fallen back into.

The thought creates an emptiness he didn't expect to feel. He feels the immense dread and loneliness he felt as a young man.

He wonders what he can do to keep the darkness away, at least until he's done. Changing his ways and being good saved him the last time; perhaps he can find a way to make amends to his soul and God while he does what he has to do. He should take an extra step to help someone. As this realization comes to him, his shaking stops, and he starts to relax.

All he needs is someone who is walking down a dark path. The rumbling of a passing train on the tracks next to the cathedral gently rocks his bed as he falls asleep.

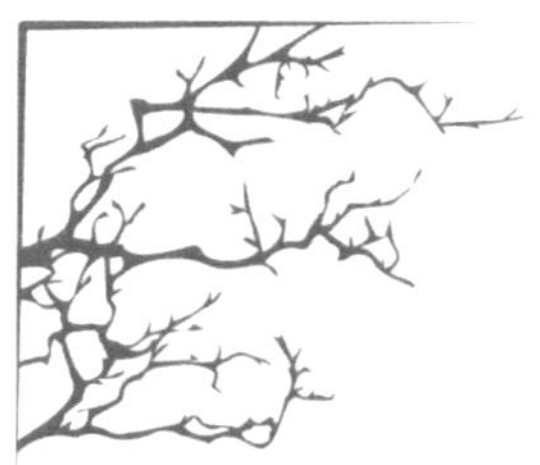

Chapter 3

Thomas Shea staggers into his mother's room at Great Lakes Alzheimer's Care Facility after another night of sitting in Shane's Lounge downing whiskey, two-fingers worth at a time, and sipping on Blue Light drafts, a Buffalo favorite among those who work in the trenches of hard-living lives.

In Thomas' case, he serves in the Buffalo Police Department's Homicide Unit. He's been working in the unit long enough to know he's ready to be done with it. The heaviness of the job has been weighing him down, and he's in need of some peace after watching shitty things happen over and over again. Sometimes it happened to people who didn't deserve it, and sometimes, they did.

He appreciates that most of the homicides he's worked on have happened to people out playing the streets and screwing around vs. random, senseless killings. Still, most of the homicides on the street are young people, and there's nothing good about young people dying or ruining their lives.

All of it takes a toll, even in the best of times.

Things have gotten worse since the night he noticed his mother having problems remembering little details she never missed. Now he wonders, as he watches her lying unconscious while hooked up to breathing and medication machines, if life would ever get any better again or is this all it has left to offer.

He sits down in the same faux leather chair he's been sitting in for months now and sets a takeout bag from the famous Anchor Bar, Home of the Wings, down on an adjustable plastic table. He kicks off his shoes, pulls a small bottle of whiskey out of his coat pocket before he tosses it onto another chair, and takes a chug. Then he opens the bag and pulls out a thin-sliced roast beef sandwich on a salted kimmelweck roll.

He sits back, half-chewing/half-sleeping, his eyes struggling to stay open while watching his mother. He appreciates that his buddy, Jim, the operator of the long-term care facility, lets him slip in and out whenever he wants. In his line of work, where he never knows what type of hours he's going to keep, the freedom to come and go helps him spend precious time with his mother while he can - even though she remains seemingly unaware of his visits.

In a short time, he's sound asleep.

Thomas' head lays over the arm of the chair as he snores away. His flip-top cell phone vibrates on the plastic table. Slowly he opens his eyes. He wipes some drool from his chin as he notices the whiskey. He takes a quick swig before he answers the phone.

"Shea here," he slowly slurs.

The voice on the other end is his partner, Kayla Harrison. A young black woman with long braided dark hair, sultry brown skin, and a gymnast's body, who's eager to be the best homicide detective Buffalo, New York, has ever produced. She grew up in the East Ferry and Wyoming Avenue neighborhood, which was ground zero for gang activity and murders at the time. She saw firsthand the fear that gets created when gang-banging teenage murderers have almost free rein over a neighborhood unable to fight back. She saw how people she loved became too scared to walk to the corner store, even during the daytime.

She also knows why gang-bangers exist; how the groups are made up of neighborhood kids who spend their days just trying to make it in places where surviving is hard. Many of these kids know hunger, loneliness, and heartbreak well. What many don't know are stable parents and homes. She feels lucky; like most families in the neighborhood, hers was a good one with loving parents who provided a safe and secure environment where she could prosper and work toward her dreams. She's always been aware of how big of a difference that made when she was a kid.

"We've got a head," she says over the phone.

"A what?"

"You know, a head: two eyes, ears, nose, mouth, set on a rounded piece of bone about the size of a bowling ball."

"Human?"

"Would I be calling if it was a doll's head?"

"I suppose not. Where?"

"Small Boat Harbor."

He wipes his eyes and brows with the palm of his left hand as he tries to clear his head.

"Okay, be down in a few."

She can hear the drunkenness in his voice. Something she's been hearing too much of over the past few months.

She knew before she took the assignment as Thomas' partner that he liked to pound back a few; he'd say it was in keeping with his Irish-Catholic background growing up in the Old First Ward. The ward was where the ships crossing the Great Lakes would come to have Irish Catholics and others off-load the grain they were carrying into towering gray elevators situated along the Buffalo River. His family settled in the ward after they escaped the famine in Ireland in the 1840s and have stayed there ever since.

The problem is Thomas has gone beyond simply pounding a few every couple of nights during happy hours. Now it's every day, and he's lasting long into the night. She's watching him fade into spiritual darkness before her eyes, and she's worried.

"Thomas?" she says.

"Yea?"

"Can you stop by Tim's and grab me a black coffee, maybe grab one for yourself? I'm buying."

She's sure he needs one.

"All right, be there soon." Thomas flips the phone shut as he looks at his mother lying motionless in the hospital bed. "Well, gotta go, mom. Be back when I can."

Thomas walks out into the dimmed yellow lights of the care center's hallway as acoustical Christmas music plays over ceiling speakers. He looks at Nurse Marcie as he makes his way past the nurse's station. He notices how gentle her face appears as she looks down at some charts. His friend had told him how much better she had made things at the facility since she arrived a couple of years ago. She's very attentive and caring and always lets him know of any changes with his mom right away. She looks up from the nurse's station desk.

"Leaving?" she asks as she looks at his bloodshot eyes, ruffled clothes, and beard-studded face.

"Yea," Thomas replies tiredly. "Gotta call."

"Don't worry, Detective. I'll keep an eye on your mom while you're gone."

"I know you will."

She smiles warmly. "It's what I'm here for."

Thomas smiles back. "Just the same, it means a lot, but I've got a favor to ask."

"What?" she responds.

Thomas pulls a vile of lavender oil out of his pocket. "If you could, when you change her linens, would you mind putting a drop or two on her pillow? Lavender is her favorite smell."

Nurse Marcie takes the vial.

"I can make sure that happens," she says. "You have a goodnight, Detective."

"Yea," Thomas says sadly as he disappears down the hallway.

Thomas takes the elevator down to the first floor and walks out the back entrance toward the parking garage across snow-covered streets. Blowing winds drive the biting cold of winter down the back of his neck as he makes his way to the old Ram pickup he's kept running for years. He had always prided himself on how well he kept it up after years of driving it over salt-covered streets during the cold months, but lately, he's been ignoring it. Now, it just sits looking dirty and dingy.

Thomas opens the driver's door and pushes take-out bags and empty cups off the front seat before he jumps in and starts it up. His breath fogs up the windshield as he waits for the engine to warm up. His thoughts turn to the case that awaits him. A head with no body.

Jesus, he thinks to himself, *what more can these sick puppies do to each other?*

He figures it's probably drug-related or domestic. In both cases, people can be exceedingly cruel to one another. Either way, he knows his job is to solve the case while dealing with people he'd rather not be around anymore. But, there's something about a bodiless head floating in the Small Bar Harbor he finds intriguing.

After stopping at Tim Horton's Donut Shop on Bailey Avenue for a couple of coffees, Thomas arrives at the entryway for the Small Boat Harbor on the outskirts of downtown Buffalo a few minutes later.

Freshly fallen snow is everywhere, and stars are shining in the dark cloudless night. He slowly drives past the Erie County Underwater Recovery team's van, numerous cop cars, and an ambulance or two until he reaches the side of the harbor where ice fishermen park by a rocky incline that goes down to the ice.

Thomas looks out at tents, portable huts, and fishermen sitting on stools by holes all over; they're trying to catch a steelhead or brown trout for dinner. Ever since he was a boy, he's always thought fishermen were crazy. In a good way, of course. It's just that he'd rather watch the action from the warmth of his vehicle than sit out in the cold or rain.

He doesn't notice Brian standing in the crowd watching as he comes to a stop.

Kayla emerges from the bright lights firefighters have set up to illuminate the marina so they can see well - much to the displeasure of the fishermen. She walks up to Thomas as he opens his driver's side door to get out. The wind off the lake blows take-out containers and cups around the inside of the cab.

Kayla gives him a worried glance.

"You're really letting things go."

He hands her a cup of coffee, ignoring the comment she just made but feeling inside like she's right.

"So, what happened?" he asks.

Kayla stares at him for a second to see if he's going to respond to what she already said.

He raises an eyebrow waiting for her response to his question.

She gives up as she grabs the coffee he gives her. She nods over to a couple of young men sitting in the back of a patrol car.

"They were the ones who found the head."

Thomas looks over at the men. "You talk to them?"

"Yea, outside of finding the head, they got nothing to add."

"How'd they find it?"

"Came down here to do some evening ice fishing, used a gas auger to drill through the ice, and when they looked down into the hole, the head popped up."

"Where's the hole?" Thomas says as he takes a sip of his coffee.

"This way."

Kayla leads Thomas down a slope of frozen grass and small boulders onto the frozen surface of the ice. Thomas looks at a heavily-clothed bearded fisherman. "How's the fishing?" he asks.

"Be better if you guys would quit walking over the ice so much. You're scaring the fish," he snarls back.

Thomas stops.

"By the way, how long have you been out here fishing?"

"Why?"

"Just wondering."

"I don't know; it was just getting dark. Around five, I guess."

"You see anything strange going on?"

"Like what?" the bearded fisherman asks as he becomes increasingly irritable.

"I don't know, maybe somebody sticking a head through a fishing hole out here."

"Wouldn't notice if they did. I've got other things to be doing than watching other fishermen unless, of course, they're catching a lot."

"Maybe we're not talking about a fisherman. Maybe we're talking about someone who looked out of place. Came out onto the ice and then left real quick."

"No, didn't see nothing like that."

Thomas hands him a card.

"Well, if you remember something, give me a ring. Okay?"

The fisherman takes the card and drops it into his tackle box.

"Yeah, sure," the bearded fisherman replies. "Now, can you move it along so we all can get back to what we came out here to do?"

"That might not be happening tonight. There's more to find, or so some think, and the Buffalo Water Recovery Team over there is getting ready to swim under the ice to find it," Thomas says as he nods toward the underwater recovery van.

"What the hell are you looking for?"

"The body that belongs to the head over there."

Thomas nods toward the hole with a towel bunched up next to it. The fisherman abruptly rises and starts packing his stuff away.

"Ah, Jesus Christ," he mumbles as Kayla and Thomas continue walking toward the head.

When they reach the hole, Kayla reaches over and removes the towel. They both look down at it.

"Anyone you know?" Thomas asks Kayla.

She looks over at Thomas and starts studying his face carefully. "Well..."

Thomas catches the twinkle in her eyes as she starts to smile. "Stop right there, young lady."

"You did ask."

"Yea, well, let's just keep it to ourselves. Okay?"

Kayla chuckles as she places the towel back over the head.

Thomas looks over at the shoreline and notices the Erie County Medical Examiner's van pulling onto the scene as underwater divers go under the ice in search of a body. The large black Ford Econoline van with paneled sides, so people can't see into the back where the bodies are carried, pulls up next to Thomas' pickup truck. Dr. James Osborne, affectionately called Ozzie by those who know him, slides out of the front passenger seat of the van and looks around at the scene.

Ozzie's a short guy, standing about five-foot-two, with a feisty temperament that gave him the gumption to rise through the ranks to master sergeant training new arrivals when he was stationed at Elmendorf Air Force Base in Alaska during the Vietnam War. He lost the tip of his nose during a training exercise that went badly up near the Arctic Circle, as well as the full use of his fingers on both hands.

The accident caused him to give up his dreams of becoming a surgeon, but it didn't stop his ability to dig around inside bodies to determine what happened to them and why. He might not be the surgeon he once hoped to be, but he enjoys the novelty of being Erie County's Medical Examiner when he's out drinking in taverns around town. There's never a shortage of people curious about meeting someone who cuts up dead people for a living. Patrons always seem ready to hear the gory stories he's willing to tell. For Ozzie, it's good for at least a few free drafts from those who'll listen.

He notices Thomas waiving and quickly descends down the slope to the ice like he's sledding on his behind. The driver of the vehicle, a much taller fellow, carefully walks down the slope behind the good doctor while carrying a black rubberized satchel.

Osborne and the driver quickly walk/slide across the ice until they reach Thomas and Kayla.

"What have we got, Tommy?" Ozzie asks in his usual jovial manner.

Thomas shoots him a "don't call me that look" as Kayla raises an eyebrow at the name. Ozzie just smiles that big shit-eating grin he generally flashes whenever he playfully ribs people.

"So far, just a head, but there's a possibility a body might be under the ice here, too." Thomas nods toward Kayla. "You remember my new partner, Kayla Harrison?"

"Oh yes, we still haven't found the time to chat. How are you, Ms. Harrison?" Ozzie replies.

"Good...and it's Detective Harrison," she says.

"Detective Harrison, it is," Ozzie says with a mischievous grin. She doesn't realize she gave him an opening for him to tease her with later on. If there's one thing he loves, it's getting under people's skin, but in a good natured way.

Ozzie looks at the towel.

"I suppose the head is under this?" he asks as he looks up at Thomas.

Thomas nods.

Ozzie squats down and removes the towel. He studies the head for a moment before rising.

"Are you done with it?"

"Pretty much," Thomas responds. "Not much I can use here."

"All right, let me get it back to the morgue so I can fully examine it. You'll let me know if they find any other parts?"

"Of course," Thomas responds.

Ozzie nods toward the towel. The driver reaches down and places the towel and the head into the black satchel he's carrying.

"Good night, Tommy," he says to Thomas before he nods at Kayla. "Detective."

Ozzie and the driver slip and slide back across the ice to the Medical Examiner's van.

Kayla turns to Thomas, "Tommy? Can I call you..."

Thomas stops her before she finishes asking, "No, you can't."

She laughs before she notices a change in him. He's suddenly growing more solemn and withdrawn as the urge to have a drink takes over.

"Well, I'll go and write up the preliminary report. Why don't you stay here in case more shows up?" he says to Kayla.

She peers into his saddening light brown eyes, "You going to be okay?"

"I'll be fine, Kayla. Really, you worry too much."

"If you say so."

"I do."

"Okay," she says as the twinkle returns to her eyes. "I'll let you know if anything else pops up."

Thomas groans. "Oh, God, you're going to have to do better than that if you plan on beating Ozzie for one-liners."

"Hey, I'm trying."

"That you are," Thomas gently laughs and softly pats her on the back. "I'll see you later."

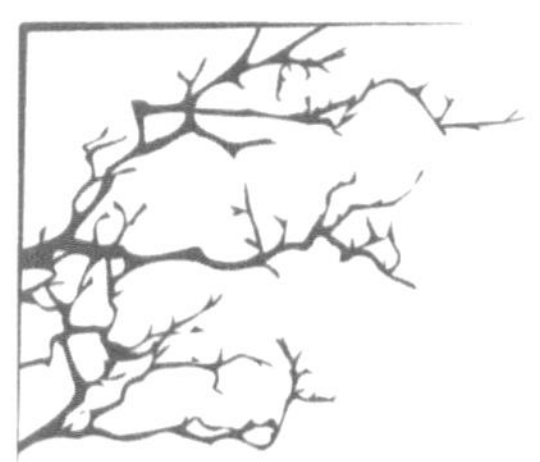

Chapter 4

Thomas pulls up the collar of his parka to stop the constant wind from blowing cold air down his back as he walks back to his pickup. He looks out over Lake Erie toward Canada when he reaches the top of the berm. Thick dark clouds filled with snow inch across open black waters toward him.

He reaches his pickup truck as clouds and snowflakes block the stars from his view. He opens the door and reaches in to grab an empty coffee cup rolling back and forth in the wind on the driver's side floor. He tosses the cup over to the passenger's side floor, jumps into the driver's seat, and starts the truck. Someone knocks on the driver's side window and shouts.

"Howdy, Thomas."

Thomas knows the voice. He turns to see Josh Wilkeson, a sixty-something reporter working the homicide beat for the Courier Express, standing at the door of his truck. He rolls down his window.

"Watcha got?" Josh asks.

"Well, Josh, we got a head. Don't have anything else at this point".

"How'd you find it?"

"Some fishermen caught it," Thomas replies.

Josh smiles like a light bulb just turned on over his head. "That'll work, for now. Thanks."

Thomas shakes his head as he watches Josh walk away. Then he slowly drives back out of the marina, past the underwater recovery team, news cameras, and dwindling crowds, and heads out onto Ohio Street to get back downtown to his office. The street takes him past the neighborhood of his youth with tall concrete grain elevators still in operation.

Driving toward Conway Park in South Buffalo, Thomas passes over train tracks that cross the street and run alongside the park until it reaches an old industrial section. He looks at the frozen grass and quiet baseball fields and remembers when his dad coached his little league team. All the kids loved his dad; he feels it's a shame he died so young. He still misses him.

Life got different back then, too. He was eight years old when his dad died, and he tried hard to become the "man of the family." It was just him and his mom until he met his future wife about five years later. Then it was him, his mom, and her. Now, soon, it will just be him. Fear rises in his gut. He wonders if he'll be able to go any further once his mom passes. Although, she's really already gone. It's just her body that he watches as he sits in his chair until she dies.

His attention comes back to the neighborhood. A different kind of sadness comes over him. So many changes happening all the time that there's no going back it seems. The Huckleberry Finn experiences of Thomas' youth, where he and his friends created trails and forts in abandoned commercial buildings and thick brush around the park, are now being replaced by condos, waterside pocket parks, docks, and entertainment venues.

About the only thing he can relate to now is the smell of Cheerios baking at the General Mills cereal plant sitting on a point of land sticking out into the Buffalo River. A smell that's been swamping the old neighborhood for generations.

Snaking around downtown streets, Thomas arrives at the back parking lot of Buffalo Police Headquarters. It's squeezed into space between the backside of the four-story cream-colored Art Deco police building and the north side of St. Joseph's Old Cathedral. He parks the car and enters the headquarters through a "Police Only" entrance off of the lot.

The squad room is typically empty this time of night, and tonight is no different. Thomas makes his way to his desk and fires up the computer. While it starts, he opens the bottom drawer on the right side of his desk and pulls out a small bottle of whiskey. He shakes the bottle as he looks inside it. Not much more than a sip is left.

Light from the clock on the steeple of the cathedral catches his eye as he twists around in his chair while downing what's left. It's 1:45 a.m., according to the placement of the hands. He sits there thinking for a moment before rising and making his way back out to the parking lot.

The tires on his pickup leave ruts in the snow that is piling up on the ground as he heads out of the lot and down the white-covered street.

Changing colors of blue, green, and red lights are shining on a band playing on the stage in the front window of Shane's, a dive bar filled with local barflies, musicians, and assorted working-class characters. The lights shine out of the window onto a decrepit patio area with broken-down railings and a picnic table holding an enraptured couple in definite need of a motel room.

Thomas gets out of his pickup in a parking lot directly across the street. He climbs over the top of growing snow mounds being pushed up by snow plows to get across the street. He steps up on the sidewalk past the couple and into the crowded and dimly lit bar.

Chris, a heavily tattooed bartender with a goatee, instantly sees Thomas and signals to him that there's an open seat around the back part of the bar near the pool table. Thomas follows his lead as he surfs his way through blurry-eyed revelers swaying their bodies and heads to the beat to a dark corner where a bar stool sits empty.

"I didn't expect to see you back tonight?" Chris shouts to him over the music.

"Nature of the beast," Thomas yells back.

"Usual?"

"Sure."

Chris quickly pours a Blue Light draft and sets it in front of him. Then he flips up a rocker glass, grabs a bottle of Old Grandad, and tilts the tip of the bottle over the glass.

"Two fingers?"

"Better make it three," Thomas replies.

"Three it is!" Chris fills the glass about halfway up and sets the bottle back behind the bar.

"We're really rockin' right now. If you need anything else, nod," Chris says as he heads toward another customer.

Thomas swirls the whiskey around before taking a long sip.

"Will do," he mumbles.

In an instant, Chris is back and sets a shot glass upside down on the bar in front of Thomas. "Next one's on Josh."

Thomas glances around the room until he finds his favorite newspaper reporter. They both raise a silent toast to each other before they down what's left in their glasses.

Later, as the music winds down and the crowd thins, Thomas sits blurry-eyed with his head bobbing up and down in the dark corner where he sits. He's aware enough to realize he's almost reached the drunken point he needs to get to in order to sleep. The point where his mind starts to shut down, and the drunkenness makes him pass out.

"You know, might be time to call it a night," Chris says as he comes up to him.

Thomas also knows now is not the time to stop. He still needs a little more time to completely shut down his mind.

"I still got three more in front of me," Thomas pushes a shot glass toward Chris. "You can start with this one."

"They can wait until another time. I'll keep track of what's owed you in the book."

Thomas just wriggles his right index finger at the glass.

"Grandad, please."

Chris knows there's no arguing with Thomas when he gets like this.

"You walking, right?"

Thomas pulls his keys out, takes off the one for his truck, and sets it on the bar for Chris to grab.

"Just pour, Chris."

Chris grabs the key and does as he's told.

Later, Thomas stumbles into the doorway of the two-story red brick apartment building he calls home. He falls into the wall of mailboxes on his right as he fumbles with the key to his apartment.

A deep sigh flows out of Thomas as he staggers into the mostly barren apartment. It's a far cry from the warm and loving home he knew just a few years ago...before one brief moment took it all away.

Moonlight glows through the grid of square panes of the front window left naked by the lack of curtains. The moonlight streams across the floor until it shines on a single chair with a stool, coffee table, and small bookcase next to it. Across from the chair in a corner by the front window is a large screen TV.

The room is littered with beer cans, takeout wrappers, and dirty clothes.

Thomas stands in the moonlight. The emptiness haunts him as he looks at the starkness of his life.

He makes his way across the living room and enters an equally barren bedroom. The moonlight shines in here, too. A ray of light shines on a picture of a woman in her thirties posing with a beautiful young 11-year-old girl. Thomas, looking clean and fit, stands behind them with his hands resting on their outward shoulders. They all smile happily together into the camera.

Thomas plops down on the bed and looks at the photo. Memories flood back to him. He grabs the photo and presses it to his chest as he falls sideways onto his bed and pillow.

His chest heaves as he lets out a primal groan. Tears start to flow. He folds into a fetal position clutching the picture. In his exhaustive drunken state, he fades into delusions.

He hears a voice echoing in his head. A young girl's voice. It's crying out in fear, "Daddy, Daddy!"

Thomas mumbles, "I'm coming. I'm coming," as sweat pours from him.

"Daddy! Daddy! It's so hot," the young voice shrieks.

"I'm coming. I'm coming," Thomas keeps mumbling until his drunkenness allows him to completely pass out.

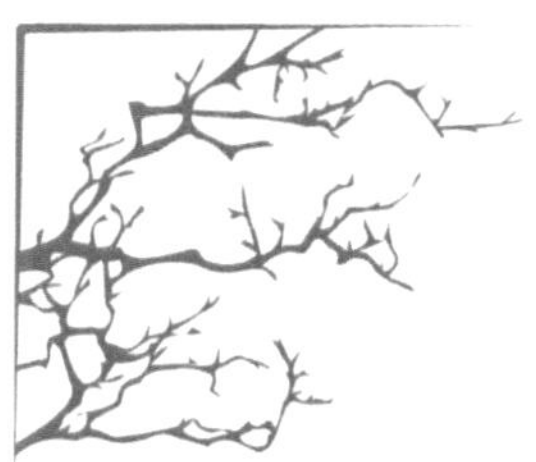

Chapter 5

Kayla pops into the entrance way of Thomas' apartment building and automatically starts to repeatedly press the buzzer to his apartment. She looks down at her feet at the Courier Express newspaper on the floor. The headline reads: "Fishermen Catch A Head Cold." She lets out a groan as she digs into her pocket for a set of keys.

She bounces up the stairs, slides a key into the door, and steps into Thomas' apartment.

The place definitely looks worse in daylight. She wonders how much longer this is going to last. She knows he's going through a deep sense of pain, but at some point, she knows, you've got to start living again, regardless of how hard that might be to do, if you want to survive.

She walks through the mess and peeks into Thomas' bedroom. He's still fully clothed, lying in the fetal position, and holding onto the picture of him with his wife and daughter.

Kayla quietly watches him looking so defeated and helpless. She hadn't personally known Thomas for long, but she was well aware of his reputation before she became his partner. He was known as the guy you came to when you had a problem, and you needed someone who would listen, help you figure out an answer, and keep the whole thing quiet when all was said and done with nothing ever to be said again. He helped many cops regain control of their lives when all seemed to be falling apart over his 23 years on the force.

He was also the one who could come onto a scene and calm everyone down. Many times he'd take a heated individual who was about to make matters worse and talk to them like a person and get

28

them to relax. He could even calm down the crackheads and dope fiends while they were jonesing.

She thought about the time before she was assigned to homicide when he showed up to a call she was on and took a mountain of a man who was threatening to kill everyone to the side and talked to him. She couldn't believe it when the mountain man laughed a little and turned around so Thomas could put the handcuffs on him. It was like they were old friends.

Thomas was made for police work. Not because he could be a badass, which he could, but because he had a good understanding of street life and what it does to people. It was his sensitivity that made him good.

Sometimes, Kayla feels part of her job is to watch that sensitivity die as he retreats into booze to escape feeling much of anything anymore.

However, a big part of her job this morning is to get him up and functioning again. She walks back across the living room and into the kitchen area. It's narrow, with a small stove and refrigerator on one side, sink and cupboards on the other, and not much room in between. She figures they pulled it from a camper and stuck it in here, or so it seems.

The stove and sink counter is filled with dirty dishes, cups, and cooking utensils.

She starts searching through the refrigerator. There are eggs, Worcestershire sauce, Bloody Mary mix, a half loaf of blue-covered moldy bread, a bottle of Frank's Hot Sauce, and some butter. He mixes the hot sauce with butter to make a tangy creamy sauce for chicken wings - which he buys by the pound at Ricardo's Puerto Rican Meats store on Niagara Street.

There's not much in the cupboards besides a box of Arm and Hammer baking soda and a package of crackers half-eaten by mice.

Kayla fishes around through the mess to find a glass that looks cleanable. She washes it out and sets it down on a sliver of open space on the counter. She puts everything she can find into it except the crackers and bread and mixes it all together. She takes it back with her into Thomas' bedroom.

Thomas hasn't budged an inch since she entered the apartment. She gives one of the bedposts a slight kick with her foot.

"Hey, Shea. Up and at 'em!" she commands.

Thomas doesn't even stir.

She kicks the post again.

Still nothing.

Kayla goes around to the end table and sets her potion down. She walks back out into the living room and spots a half-empty takeout beverage container next to the chair.

She grabs the cup and walks into the kitchen. She pours what's left in the container into the sink, rinses it out, and half-fills it with water.

She goes back into the bedroom and stands near Thomas' head. Gently easing the picture from his grasp; she sets it on the end table next to her potion. Sadness fills her face as she looks at the happy family that once was.

Then she turns and starts dripping water from the container down onto Thomas' face.

Thomas slaps at the droplets landing on his face as he slowly awakens, realizing all is not well. He sits straight up and scowls at Kayla.

"What the hell are you doing?" he barks.

"Waking you up like you told me in the message you left," she says.

"By pouring water on my face?"

"Hey, it worked, didn't it?"

"Oh, for Christ's..." Suddenly, Thomas feels a little wobbly. She notices his face changing colors and steps away from him.

"I assume you remember where the bathroom is?" she says half-jokingly.

Thomas shoots her a "shut up" look as he staggers to his feet and quickly heads to the bathroom.

She hears the toilet flush. Thomas comes back into the doorway. His head is sweaty, and he looks like he's ready to drop dead.

"Here, drink this first to wake up."

"You can be such a pain in the..."

"Drink!" she interrupts.

Thomas smells the concoction and pulls his nose back.

"What is this?" he asks.

"Something my grandmother taught me to make for granddad on Sunday mornings before church. It's good. Drink it."

Thomas gives her a skeptical trusting look before downing a third of the glass. He immediately grabs his stomach and convulses.

"By the way," Kayla says with a bit of sick satisfaction, "I'm not sure how old the eggs were. You might be puking again in about twenty minutes."

He gasps, "My God, you trying to kill me?" .

"Why? You need some help?" she replies.

He flashes her a dirty look as he rushes back into the bathroom again and slams the door shut behind him.

Kayla can hear him heaving his guts out once more. She yells through the door, "You might want to shower while you're in there. You smell like a brewery."

She grabs the newspaper, sits down in the chair in the living room, and listens as Thomas quits heaving and the shower goes on.

In a short time, Thomas reappears fully clothed with a head full of wet hair.

Kayla yells over to him.

"Ozzy should be completing the post on the head soon. Ready to go over?" she asks.

"Yea," Thomas replies, "Just let me get some water."

Thomas ducks into the kitchen. He turns on the faucet and rattles some glasses before reaching under the sink and grabbing a bottle of

Old Grandad. Quickly, he opens the lid, pours three fingers' worth into a dirty coffee cup, and puts the bottle back under the sink.

Kayla walks into the doorway as Thomas downs the hefty shot.

"C'mon, Thomas," she pleads.

Thomas calmly sets the cup into the sink.

"Don't give me grief, Kayla. It's only a quick boost to make me feel better."

"If you did less, you wouldn't need a boost."

"No lecturing, okay?"

She looks deeply into his eyes. "I'm worried," she replies.

"No need. Remember, I'm Irish."

"There's a limit to that."

Thomas forces a smile, "Which I haven't reached yet".

Kayla looks disgusted, "Yea, sure. Let's just get to the morgue".

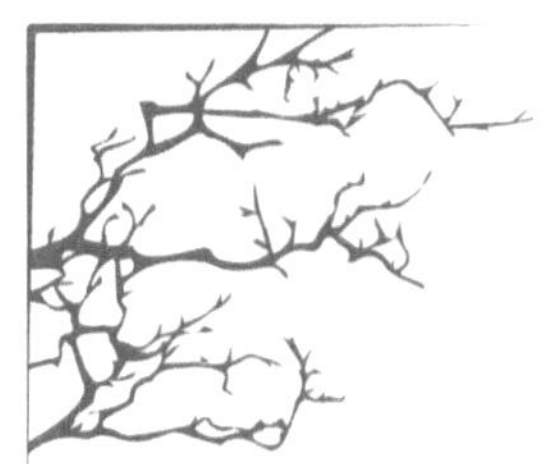

Chapter 6

Brian opens his eyes as he lies flat on his back and stares up at the ceiling. He thinks about what's been happening to him over the past few days. He feels strange. He knows what he did was wrong, but it brought him a certain exhilaration knowing he finally stood up again and did what he thought should be done.

An exhilaration he has known before and knows how dangerous it is to feel.

In some ways, he feels like an old friend has returned and agrees with what he has done...and with what he still has to do. But, he also feels a tinge of guilt - a tinge he hoped he'd never feel again. The old battle is beginning to rage again in his soul. That battle between good and evil he has faced his whole life. He reflects about how the battle led him to the Cathedral's doors and into the warm embrace of Father Isaiah.

Fear rises up in him. Coming here and helping out made him feel special and gave him a tremendous purpose. Over time, he went from a street kid to a young man who was gaining respect and acceptance in the community. Good people who wanted nothing more than to see him do well invited him into their homes. He knows he helped people. He knows he helped Jennifer.

"Ah, Jennifer. Sweet Jennifer," he says to himself. He knows he helped her when she finally smiled after weeks of trying to get through to her. He knew what she was going through. What she had done and what had been done to her. He knew the type of life she lived often destroyed the soul and mind, but the one thing he didn't know was how she had captured his heart.

In a very simple way, she became his world. She was all he could think about, and he would get so excited when he knew he was going to see her that day. An excitement he hadn't felt since he was a boy, and he was shocked he was feeling it again.

He loved her soft blue eyes. He had found a home in them.

The rage just builds until the old Brian takes over again. The one who thinks in terms of revenge and setting the record straight. This is the Brian he needs to be right now.

A burst of energy takes over. He jumps into the shower to get ready for the day. As he touches his body, his skin tingles as his hands move up and down his chest, thighs, and places in between. Suddenly, he becomes aware of how long it's been since his skin tingled. Since he really felt the steam of hot water warming his neck.

He feels like he has a purpose again. Not one of hiding and pretending to be someone he's not, but of one when he was younger, full of life and, at times, full of death. A time when he felt in control and not controlled by the thoughts and actions of others.

There are parts of his plan he still has to figure out, but he feels confident things will be okay. All he knows now is he has a mission to complete, and the determination he sees in his eyes as he looks in the bathroom mirror tells him he's ready.

He smiles at his reflection.

"Hi, old friend," he says to himself, "Time to play."

In the back of his mind, though, a faint voice tells him what he's doing is wrong and he needs to find a way to balance his evilness with goodness. If he doesn't, he knows other ghosts from his past will return to damn his soul to hell. The voice tells him he must find a way to atone for what he's doing.

But the voice doesn't tell him how to atone. He must figure that part out for himself.

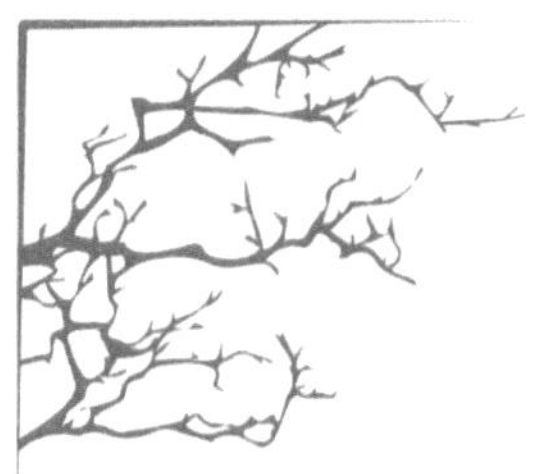

Chapter 7

Ozzie stands on a stool to get high enough above the stainless steel autopsy table to be able to look down on the decapitated head. A large operating room light shines on it so he can get a good look at things.

He seems particularly intrigued by markings on a couple of vertebrae connected to the bottom of the skull when Thomas and Kayla walk in.

"Did you know some people believe you maintain awareness if you get your head cut off before you completely lose consciousness and die?" Ozzie says without looking up from the table.

"No, I did not know that," Thomas replies.

"Yep, there's a story about when Marie-Anne Charlotte de Corday d'Armont, affectionately known as Charlotte Corday to those who loved or hated her, I forget which, had her head lopped off by a guillotine for killing Jean-Paul Marat, a defender of poor people during the French Revolution. After her head fell into a basket, it was picked up by Francois le Gros. He slapped both cheeks on her face to further dishonor her, and people in attendance said her face grew angry after he did it," Ozzie explains.

He continues as he looks up.

"Recent studies have shown that brain activity can last for up to half an hour after the heart has stopped beating. Some say you stay conscious during this time but are unable to let people know."

Kayla steps up around Ozzie to get a better, more intimate view of what he's doing.

Thomas pulls his cell phone out of his pocket, he's seen enough of this type of stuff before, and there's really no reason to look at more. "I'm going to step out and make a call while you guys dissect the body," he says as they seemingly ignore him.

"One of the things you want to determine," Ozzie says to Kayla as he pushes esophageal and bronchial tissue away from the bone with a trimming knife specially made for performing autopsies, "is the type of weapon used during a murder. In this case, I've made the determination that a hunting, military, or survival knife was likely used."

"How do you know?" Kayla asks

"Come closer, Ms. Harrison, and I'll show you why."

"That's Detective Harrison," she says as she steps in next to Ozzie and looks down at the severed head.

Ozzie smiles.

"A couple of things," Ozzie perks up as he starts to explain. "Do you see the slices in the bone?"

Ozzie points out slices on the vertebrae attached to the bottom of the skull.

Kayla nods her head yes.

"They were done by a very sharp knife meant to cut through joints, cartilage, and bone, like when you dress a deer while hunting in the woods. Another thing, the way the neck was cut, there aren't a lot of carving marks through the meaty portion of it - it was pretty much a straight cut with minimal stopping. It takes a strong knife to do this. That rules out kitchen and surgical knives," Ozzie points out. "However, to make a more certain determination of the knife, I would need to examine a stab wound made by the knife to take measurements of the blade and its angles. There aren't any stab wounds here but there might be some on the body if we can find it."

"What about all these wounds to his face and scalp?" Kayla wonders as she studies the dead man's face.

"Postmortem. Likely caused by his head scraping along the bottom of the ice as it moved around in the water," Ozzie replies.

Kayla takes the information in.

"You think we'll find the body?" she asks.

"It might take a little while, but if it's in the water like the head was and sunk, it will fill up with gas as it decomposes. Once it fills, it should float to the top of the water if it doesn't get stuck under the ice floes. Alternatively, the body could be floating above the water now if the lungs are still full of air. Either way, it'll show up," Ozzie says with confidence.

Thomas talks quietly into his cell phone in an isolated part of the hallway. "How's she doing, Nurse Marcie?"

"We've just cleaned her and changed the linen."

"Again, I want you to know how much I appreciate you being there."

"Thank you. Detective. Oh, and I remembered to put some lavender on her pillowcase."

"Thanks again," he says warmly.

A little bit of solitude captures his heart as he hangs up his phone. *At least my mom is being taken care of well, better than the shit that's going on out here,* he contemplates before heading back into the autopsy room.

Ozzie stands up straight on the stool as Thomas walks back into the room.

"How's your mother doing?" Ozzie asks.

Thomas glances over at him.

"Can't get anything past you, can I?" Thomas says.

"Sometimes...but how's she doing?"

"No change."

Ozzie and Thomas share a look that says both are grieving and no more needs to be said.

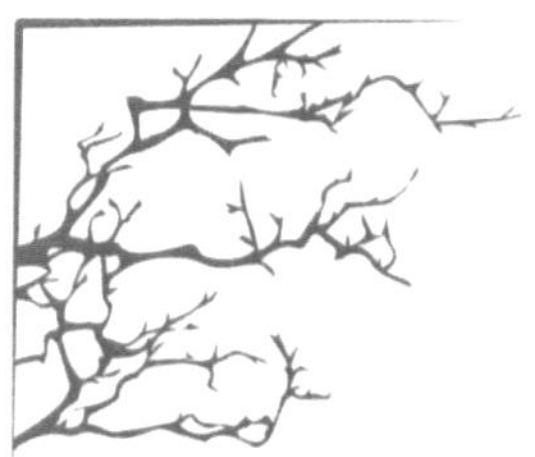

Chapter 8

When Thomas and Kayla walk into the squad room at Police Headquarters, they are greeted by a Buffalo-styled meticulously groomed man. His beard is combed and fully flows down to his chest, he wears clean insulated ankle-high work boots, and his plaid shirt is tucked neatly inside his Carhartt jacket. He looks like the type of man you'd see clearing snow for others after a big storm with his big ass snowblower before going out for a couple of beers with his buddies.

Thomas instantly recognizes him as the fisherman on the ice.

"You clean up nice," Thomas says.

"Yea," the fisherman responds. "Say, I, um, want to apologize for being such a hard ass on the ice. It's just, I wait so long for this moment when the dead of winter hits and the ice really freezes so I can get out there, and it really only lasts for a few weeks. People walking back and forth over the ice disturb the fish and they won't bite, and, I don't know, I take the time doing that seriously. Anyway, I'm sorry."

"No need. When I was a boy, my dad would take me out on the ice to fish. I get it," Thomas replies. "So, what brings you in?"

"I remembered something from a couple of nights ago," the fisherman replies. "A guy in a long black coat threw a round object into the water when I arrived to go fishing that night. That object could have been a head."

"Where did he throw it from?" Kayla asks.

"From the end of Gallagher's Pier. I noticed him because I liked how his long coat fluttered in the wind; he looked like a character from that Keanu Reeves movie," the fisherman struggles to remember.

"The Matrix?" Thomas offers.

"Yea, the Matrix. Where his long coat swings around as bullets pass by his head. Cool stuff. Anyway, I thought you should know."

Thomas shakes his hand.

"Thanks. By the way, what's your name?"

"Jason Krull, I work at Sister's Hospital in the Maintenance Department."

"If we have any more questions, can we reach you there?" Kayla asks.

"Um, yea, but I could also give you my number."

"That works," Thomas says. "What is it?"

The fisherman jots his personal information down on a pad and leaves.

Thomas looks at Kayla.

"We should probably check it out before the weather changes," he says.

"Sounds good to me," Kayla says as she shuts off her computer and grabs her coat.

When they get to Gallagher's Beach, Thomas has to swerve around a city plow truck coming out of the parking lot as he and Kayla pull into it. They drive until they pull up to the base of the wooden pier, and get out of the pickup truck. Stepping over the snow mounds left by the snowplow, they walk out onto the pier. The first thing they notice is drag marks and a trail of blood in the snow.

"Well, it looks like a large sack was dragged through here. Could have been a body," Thomas says to Kayla.

At the end of the pier, a section of snow is gone from the railing. Thomas walks over and looks over the side. He sees blood marks along the outside of the rail.

"The fisherman was right. It looks like he saw something get thrown from here, and that something might be what we're looking for," Thomas says.

"Looks like," Kayla replies.

"But I don't think this is the murder scene."

"Why not?"

"Not enough blood. Plus, the way the blood is spilled, it looks like it pumped out a little at a time. Like every time he pulled on the body, blood would gush out of the wounds. I'd say he was decapitated somewhere else, and the head and body were brought here to dump them in the water."

Thomas studies the scene some more.

"Well, let's call it in and have the crime scene techs come out to collect blood samples and whatever else they can find," he says.

When they get back to the entrance of the pier, Thomas follows the trail of blood in the patted down snow out onto the parking lot. He looks disappointingly at the freshly plowed surface.

"Would have been nice to have some tire marks left," Thomas says.

"Why?"

"You can use them to track down the type of car someone drives. You won't always get an exact match, but anything to narrow down the scope of an investigation helps."

Thomas and Kayla jump back into the pickup truck and head back out onto Route 5 to take the lake route back downtown. They don't notice that the plow didn't remove snow in front of the entrance to the grain elevator or the tire tracks left in it.

Thomas' phone vibrates as he heads along Route 5 toward the Skyway that takes people over the Buffalo River and ship canals into downtown. He pulls over to the side and answers it.

"Shea, here," he says as he answers it. He listens for a moment. 'Got it."

He turns to Kayla, "They found a headless floater near Ontario Street".

In minutes, Thomas and Kayla pull into the parking lot at the end of Ontario Street, about nine miles downriver from Gallagher Beach.

They get out and walk over to the crowd to watch as the Buffalo Fire Department's fire boat, Edward M. Cotter, breaks up ice near and around the launch. The fire boat, built way back in 1900, is the only boat in Buffalo that can handle the frozen waters of Niagara River this time of year. After the boat nudges its bow into the eddy around the launch pad to break up the ice, it then circles back out into the water to get behind the headless body.

A powerful water cannon mounted on the bow of the boat fires up. At first, a little stream trickles out of the canon, and then *boom!* Suddenly, the cannon produces a powerful stream and a foggy mist. The mist gets swept up in the cold wind blowing across the river and lands on those on the ramp. Thomas and Kayla both turn away as the freezing water and cold sting their faces. They walk to another position where they can watch what's going on without water getting on them.

The firefighters direct the stream so it hits the water just in front of the body to create a plowing effect. The powerful stream pushes the body through the broken-up ice towards the ramp. Within moments, firefighters grab it and place it in a thick black rubber body bag on a stretcher.

Thomas and Kayla walk over. Thomas motions to one of the firefighters. "Mind if I look things over?" he asks.

"No problem, Thomas" the firefighter says as he steps away from the body.

Thomas starts checking the pockets until he finds what he's looking for. He pulls a wallet out of one of the back pockets and opens it. He removes a driver's license and looks at Kayla.

"Might have caught a break. ID," he says as he holds up the license.

"That helps," Kayla replies.

"Sure does." Thomas motions to the firefighter. "I'm done, thanks."

The firefighter tucks the body into the bag and zips it up. Thomas and Kayla start walking toward the pickup truck.

"Well, we've got to make sure the body belongs to the same person as the one on the driver's license," he says to Kayla. "It'll probably take a day or two before Ozzie gets the information he'll need to make a positive identification."

"What do we do until then?" Kayla asks.

"Wait," Thomas says as he jumps into the pickup truck and starts it up.

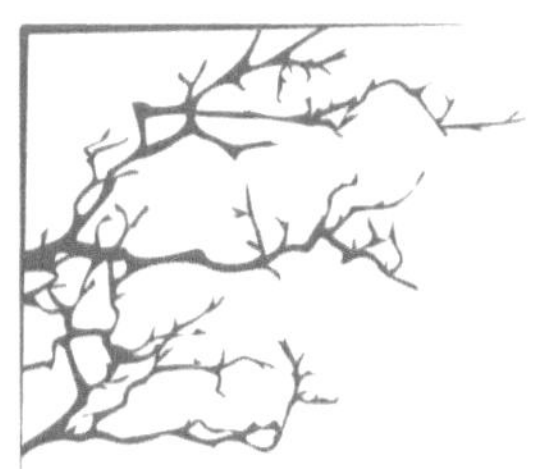

Chapter 9

Sun shines through the window of Thomas' mother's room on this bright winter day. He sits perched on the faux leather chair he's been watching her from day after day and night after night. Today, though, he's got more on his mind than his mother, or even having a drink. There's something about Gallagher's Beach that's bothering him.

He feels like he missed something.

Before long, he's up and out of the chair and in his pickup truck, heading back to the beach.

When he arrives, he parks alongside Route 5 and looks out over the whole beach environment before he drives into the parking lot. He's disappointed nothing is sticking out for him. He puts the pickup in gear and enters the parking lot. As he drives past the entryway for the grain elevator, he notices tire tracks under a layer of softly fallen snow going to the monolithic structure.

The pickup comes to a crawl as he looks at the tracks going right up to the front doors. *Might as well check it out,* he thinks, *since there's nothing else to go on.*

The first thing that comes to mind is the need to protect the tire tracks in case something does show up. So, he parks his pickup on the plowed section of the parking lot and walks through the snow toward the elevator. As he gets close to the front door, he sees where the tire tracks end. There's a lot of disturbance in the snow all around one portion of the tracks and frozen puddles of blood.

Walking around the top of the tracks, he makes his way to the front doors of the elevator. The doors bang against the chain each time the wind blows. It's the only thing keeping them from blowing wide open and knocking him to the ground as he gets near them. He sees blood puddled around at the base of the door and on the handles, chain and lock.

He pulls on the lock to see if it will open, but he has no such luck.

He feels a warm breeze filter in off the lake and realizes the temperatures are starting to rise above freezing for the afternoon. He knows he must act quickly to preserve the tracks before they melt.

Within moments, he's back at his pickup truck digging through a pile of junk and clothes filling the area behind the front seat and back wall. Frustration builds up; he can't find what he's looking for. He silently screams at himself *"When am I going to stop doing this shit!"*

He knows when, as he feels the weight of a small bottle in his inside coat pocket, *he knows damn well when!*

Pulling out his cell phone, he calls Kayla.

"What's up, Thomas," she says as she answers.

"You at the office?" he asks.

"Yea."

"Good, I need you to grab the tripod and satchel by my desk," he says. "Oh, and bring bolt cutters."

"Why? Where are you?"

"Back at Gallagher Beach. I think I've found something, but I don't have my damn equipment. How warm is it supposed to get today?"

"Um...34 degrees."

"Good, that gives us a little time."

"For what?"

"Preserve evidence. Hurry."

Thomas ends the call as he looks around. Feelings of disgust rise in him as he realizes his sloppy behavior is really affecting his work. It disgusts him so much he takes out that small bottle he has hidden inside his jacket pocket and takes a swig to calm his thoughts. Then he heads back to the elevator to see if there's anything he can see from the outside.

He walks around the elevator but nothing's sticking out.

Kayla pulls up with lights flashing as he returns to the front of the grain elevators.

Thomas smiles to himself, *Well, I did say make it quick.*

She comes to a stop next to his pickup, gets out, and opens the trunk to the aging Chevrolet Caprice she checked out from the yard.

"I got here as fast as I could," she says as Thomas walks up.

"I'm impressed," Thomas responds.

Kayla motions to the trunk. "I brought what you said. What we got?"

"Blood and drag marks up by the grain elevator's front doors," Thomas replies as he points at the concrete structure before nodding at the tire tracks.

"Those tire tracks lead up to the doors," he adds. "So, before we disturb anything and before the snow melts, we're going to preserve what we can. You ever taken casts and photos before?"

Kayla shakes her head no.

He reaches into his truck and grabs a camera case he was able to dig out.

"Grab the satchel," Thomas instructs. "Be careful not to step on the tracks, okay? I'll go over how to do it this time and you can do it the next time. You good with that?"

"Sounds good," Kayla says as she grabs the bag and trudges behind him through the snow.

Walking slowly beside the tracks, Thomas looks for indentations that really stick out and clearly show tread marks. Finding a suitable location, he sets up the tripod and camera.

"The first thing we want to do is take images of the tread marks," Thomas says. He places the tripod next to the tracks and attaches his camera do it. He pulls out a film canister and puts the film into the camera.

"Film?" Kayla asks.

"Yea, it still works. No need to change it until it doesn't work anymore."

"Been awhile since I've seen one."

Thomas ignores her as he gets down on his knees and gently blows the light snow out of the tracks under the camera.

"You want to get snow and leaves out of the image zone as best you can without disturbing anything," Thomas says as he grabs a regular-sized can of gray spray paint out of the satchel.

"We put down a light layer of paint to help bring out the details of the tread in the images," Thomas says as he sprays paint over the tread marks.

He then reaches into the bag and pulls out a dark L-shaped one-by-two-foot framing square and presses it down in the snow until it reaches the same level as the tire tracks.

"We use this so you can scale the images in the photos."

He gets up and attaches a remote control device to the camera.

"I use a remote control so I don't have to touch the camera to activate it while taking photos," Thomas explains.

"Why?" Kayla asks.

"When you touch the camera, even to press the button, it tends to shake it a little. That causes blurriness in the image. With the remote control, I don't touch the camera so the camera doesn't shake. So, the images come out clearer and more defined," Thomas says as he snaps off a series of images.

"Okay, now the tracks," Thomas says.

"From the snow?"

"Yep." Thomas grabs a bag of powder out of the satchel, "We use stuff called Dental Stone."

"Dental stone?" Curiosity fills Kayla's face.

"Yea, Dentists use it for kind of the same thing we do, to make molds and casts; only we use it to make casts of footprints and tracks in snow and mud. Works great."

Thomas hands Kayla a gallon-sized plastic freezer storage bag.

"Here, open this," he says.

Kayla opens the bag wide. Thomas measures out four cups, one at a time, of dental stone and pours it in.

"Now we need really cold water to mix in so it doesn't heat up too fast while curing," Thomas says as he takes the bag from Kayla.

Kayla points toward the lake.

"Will lake water do?" she asks.

"As long as it's clean. I've got a couple of cups in the pickup we can use."

"No? Really?" she says sarcastically.

Thomas gives her a "don't be a smart-ass look."

Kayla laughs, "I'll go grab the cups."

"I'll meet you down by the water," he sneers, jokingly, back.

Thomas steps carefully along the ice to make sure he doesn't fall through while creeping toward the edge where it's thinner. He uses the heel of his boot to chip a hole in the ice to dip the cups in that Kayla's carrying over.

She hands one cup at a time to Thomas. He dips each one into the water to fill it up a bit, swirls the water around until it picks up the coffee grounds at the bottom, and tosses it out leaving the cup clean. Then he dips the cup in one more time while being very careful not to let leaves, twigs, or anything else float into it. He hands it back to Kayla. She hands him the second cup and he repeats the process.

Once both cups are filled, they go back to the track marks.

Thomas pours the water into the zipper bag and seals it. He starts squeezing the bottom of the bag where the powder has settled. "You want to squeeze the powder to break up the chunks. Kind of like how you break up the batter to make pancakes light and airy," he says with a grin. "I'm sure your grandmother told you that when you made breakfast for good ole' granddad."

A sheepish smile crosses her face.

Finally, he seems satisfied the mixture is complete. "Now, all we have to do is gently pour the solution into the tracks and let it set."

"How long does that take?" Kayla asks.

Thomas looks around to get a good sense of the weather.

"I'd say about 45 minutes to an hour."

"What'll we do 'til then?"

"I'm glad you asked", Thomas says. "Now, we do the same with the footprints by the front doors."

Thomas has Kayla repeat the process of taking pictures and casts of the left and right shoe prints. He nods his head in approval as she gets everything right.

"Alright, time for some exploring," Thomas says. "Did you bring the bolt cutters?"

"Back seat."

"Good, grab 'em while I put this stuff away. Will you?"

"Sure thing."

Moments later, Kayla meets Thomas at the front doors of the elevator carrying the bolt cutters. He points out the blood and markings.

"I think we might find something in here," he says as he grabs the bolt cutters and cuts the chain in half.

Kayla looks at him. "Um, aren't we supposed to get a warrant before we cut a chain and enter?"

Thomas grabs the chain and lock, walks to the edge of the land, and tosses them far into the water past the ice collecting along the shore's edge. He walks back.

"What chain?" he replies.

With nothing to hold the door handles together, the wind blows them open.

"Oh, look, the door's open!" Thomas sticks his head in and notices a trail of blood along the floor. "And it looks like we have reason to believe a crime has been committed here. There might even be someone in need of help. Listen, I think I hear a moan."

"That's the wind," Kayla responds.

"Can't be sure. Need to check it out."

Thomas enters and follows the blood trail into the interior bowels of the elevator. As he walks, the bravado he just exhibited to Kayla slowly drains out of him. A sense of dread starts to build. He starts thinking about how many times he's followed trails to find something he'd rather not see. Hell, he's done it so much, he can't even remember all the times. Faces of the dead that he thought he would never forget don't seem to come to him anymore – while others never seem to go away.

The trail leads into a narrow dark hallway going back to the abandoned office area of the elevator. Thomas follows the blood until he comes to a closed office door.

He reaches for the handle.

For a moment, every ounce of his body screams *don't turn it*. He wants to listen to the voice...but he knows he can't.

He turns the handle and pushes the door open. Complete darkness fills the room. He grabs his cell phone and hits the flashlight button. The place lights up.

Blood is everywhere on and around an empty cold metal chair in the middle of the room. He closes his eyes and takes a breath. The putrid smell of rotting blood fills his nostrils.

"I think we've found something," he says, resigned to the fact that this shit really never does get any better.

Kayla looks in. "I think you're right." She notices the change in Thomas. "You okay?"

"Yea, let's call it in."

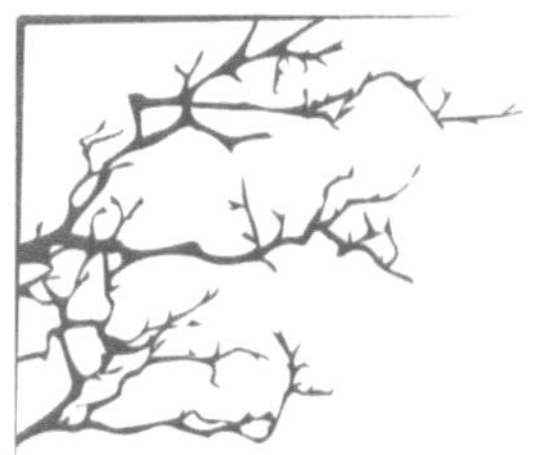

Chapter 10

Ozzie is back at the autopsy table standing on his stool when Thomas and Kayla return to the morgue.

"Has the DNA match between the head and body been completed yet?" Thomas asks him.

"I've sent the material in, but it's going to take a little while longer," Ozzie replies, "However, I don't think we'll need it to confirm identity through DNA at this point."

"Why not?" Kayla asks.

"Mere observation, my dear, Ms. Harrison," Ozzie replies.

"Detective Harrison," she says, a little more demanding now.

"Indeed. Well, Detective, there are a few things that allow one to make an educated determination if the head belongs to the body. The first is that it was separated between the C2 and C3 vertebrae. The C2 is still connected to the bottom of the skull while the corresponding C3 is attached to the body. Both show signs of using the same cutting tool on the bone parts. You can also see where the blade finally went through the intervertebral disk which acts as a cushion between vertebrae. The halves of the disk are still connected to each vertebra.

"Another sign is the deterioration of the skin on the head and body both appear to be at the same rate of decomposition including the color and condition of the skin.

"Plus", Ozzie said with a twinkle in his eyes, "We were able to confirm through the use of fingerprints and dental records the two sections make up one singular body. Once we knew the name from the ID in the wallet, it was easy doing the rest."

"So, in other words, you made a solid ID and you don't really need to do a DNA test?" Thomas asks after watching Ozzie give another learning experience to the new homicide detective.

"Very perceptive, Tommy," Ozzie says. "Your dad would be proud."

"Ozzie, could you not call me that?" Thomas almost pleads.

"Tommy, I knew your dad and mother before you were born and I played with you on my knee. You'll always be Tommy to me," Ozzie replies with a wink.

"I get that and I appreciate the memories, but you've got to stop with the 'Tommy' stuff. At least when we're not alone."

Ozzie produces one of his famed smiles.

"However, I did find something unusual," Ozzie states as he changes the subject back to the body.

"What's that?" Thomas asks.

"The lack of defensive or offensive wounds. There's a series of scratches and cuts on the body, but they're minor and could be the result of someone moving the body or the ice floes causing damage to it after death. I think he was subdued by something first and then killed. I sent tissue samples over to toxicology to test for poisons and medicines but it won't be done for at least a few days."

Thomas looks over at Kayla.

"You ready to get back? We gotta look up the background on this guy."

She is amazed at what she is seeing on the autopsy table and is taking it all in.

"Kayla!" Thomas snaps.

She looks up with her head cocked.

"What?" she replies.

"Ready to go back to the office?"

"Umm, yea, sure," she responds.

"Well," Ozzie looks at Thomas, "Let me know if you find a next of kin so I can arrange a positive ID."

"Will do, Oz," he replies.

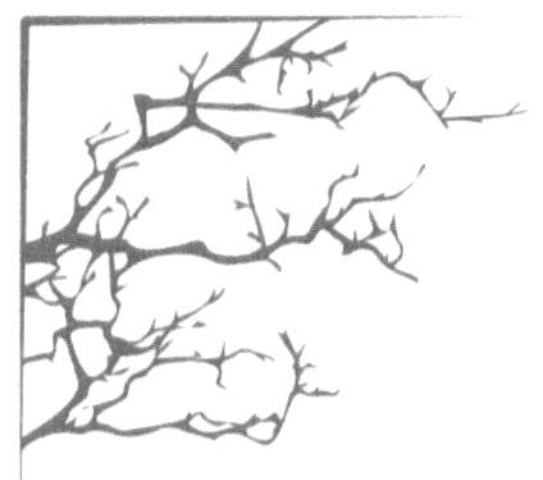

Chapter 11

Hardly anyone noticed the late dark blue Subaru Outback pulling into the parking lot near the sledding hill at Chestnut Ridge County Park. From his vantage point, Brian can see the tall slopped chutes designed to give tobogganists and sledders an extra power boost as they surge down the snow-packed hill covered with ice.

He can also see those coming in and out of the lodge building in front of him and the maintenance shed down at the end of the parking lot along tall pines to his right. He figures if Troy Englewood works here, he'll be able to see him walking around at some point from this spot.

He pulls out a thermos and pours himself a hot cup of green tea and sinks back into his seat for what he expects might be a long wait.

A wait that takes longer than expected.

The morning gray skies give way to the bright skies of midday before Brian starts wondering if the information he gathered from looking at Troy's son's Facebook posts was wrong. Maybe Troy doesn't work here.

He thinks he'll have to be more active in his reconnaissance.

He looks into the rear-view mirror to make sure the fake beard and mustache he put on this morning still look good. It really doesn't, but he's satisfied his disguise is holding up. He puts on his dark sunglasses, pulls his dark wool bucket cap down over his forehead, and exits his Subaru.

Brian meanders into the crowd at the top of the sledding hill while keeping a constant eye out for Troy. Although, he does stop to admire

Buffalo's downtown skyline 20 miles away and the mist rising from Niagara Falls behind it in the background before entering the lodge.

The lodge is full of families with kids and young and old lovers alike. They sit at long thick wooden tables near a roaring fire in the large stone fireplace at one end of the building. The air is full of merriment and glad tidings, except for what Brian has in his heart. The type of merriment he seeks is far different from what families and lovers seek.

Brian inspects nearly every inch as he wades through the crowd looking for the familiar face he's come here to see, but the face is nowhere to be found. Feeling a little discouraged, he approaches Debbie, a pretty young blonde-haired girl working the concession stand.

"Hi, I'm looking for Troy Englewood. He's an old friend of mine and I heard he was working here," Brian asks.

"Oh, he does, but he's off today," she replies.

"Really?" Brian says sweetly, "Just by chance, when does he work?"

"He's the late-shift guy. He's usually here just before three Tuesday through Saturday and works until ten cleaning things up and making repairs. He's a very nice man."

Sure he is, Brian thinks to himself, but not nice or wise enough to escape what's coming.

"You want to leave a message?"

"No, that's not necessary," Brian replies. "I'll just stop back. I guess he'll be working tomorrow night?"

"Sure will."

"What time does everything close up around here?"

"The park closes around seven and we're usually gone about an hour later."

"Well, thank you."

"You don't want anything?" she asks.

"Not right now. I'll stop back later, though."

"Good. I'll see you then," she says in a wonderfully happy youthful way.

BRIAN SMILES AT HER as he turns and walks away.

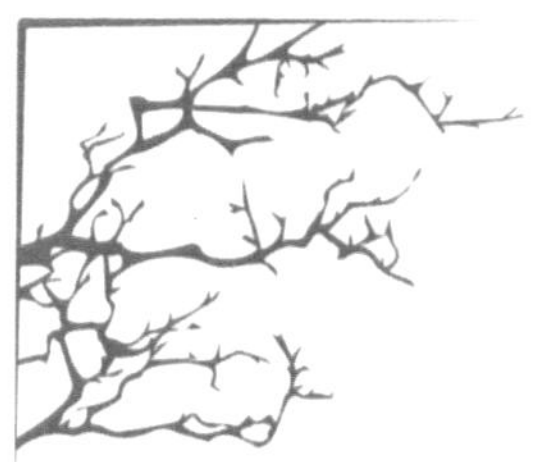

Chapter 12

Thomas stares out of his office window at the stained glass window of the Holy Family set into side of the old cathedral next door. It makes him think about when he had a family while Kayla gleefully types the last keys into the computer and hits send.

"Voila!" she beams.

"Watcha got?" Thomas asks.

"Theodore Casey, 398 Norwood Avenue here in the city. Says here he's a veteran who belonged to the 10th Mountain Division based out of Watertown. Served as a non-medical counseling resource officer and now works, or did, at the Black Rock Prison for Women."

"Anything else?"

Kayla shakes her head. "No, doesn't have any type of criminal record and I don't see anything coming up for civil complaints. He seems like a good man who served his country, came home, and settled in. He had a nice ordinary life from what I can see."

"Well, we'll see about that. Good people don't generally get their heads cut off and tossed into the water."

Kayla cocks her head. "True, but so far, there's nothing here."

Thomas rises from his chair. "Well, we might as well find out. What's the address again?"

"398 Norwood Avenue."

"Alright," Thomas says with as much enthusiasm as he can muster - which isn't much. "Let's check it out."

Kayla looks at him like she's watching a young man turn into an old man right before her eyes. She stops.

"You know, Thomas, I know I don't really know you a lot, but I know you a little bit. I'm worried."

God, I'm worried myself, he thinks, *I'm friggin' fallin' apart here and I can't stop it!*

He looks at the concern in her eyes.

"I'm fine," he says as he grabs his coat and heads out the door.

Tall maple and oak trees devoid of leaves cast the shadows of large branches over the front of the Victorian homes filled with kids playing in the sun and snow as Thomas and Kayla drive down Norwood Avenue. They pull up in front of a house painted in soft hues of blue, green, and yellow. The number 398 on the porch banister is painted as bright flowers.

This is an artist's house with a feminine touch, and it ignites a slight yearning for softness in Thomas's soul. He's reminded of the innocence he once knew and lost, and he realizes all too well he's coming here to end the innocence of someone who looks like they have a beautiful soul. Regret fills his heart and makes it hard to open the door to his pickup to get out, but he fights through it and gets out along with Kayla. They walk up the porch steps and stand at the front door. Thomas reaches out and presses the doorbell.

They turn to watch a young mother grab up her children from the snow pile in the front yard to take them into the house next door. She notices Thomas and Kayla looking at her.

"Hi," she says, "You looking for Shelly?"

"Would that be Ms. Casey?" Kayla asks.

"Used to be. She's normally in the backyard this time of year and she probably can't hear you out front here."

Thomas and Kayla come down off the porch and walk around to the side of the house to get to the backyard. The houses in this part of town were built close together in the early 1900s as there wasn't yet a need for wide driveways and garages for cars in those days.

The walk back is filled with artistic statues, decorative metal benches, and various flower pots sitting empty until spring. There is a flair for everything.

They reach a wooden fence door and open it.

Inside the yard, they notice several completed ice sculptures twinkling in the sun. Then they notice Shelly working on a piece of a winged eagle in flight with a rabbit clenched in its talons near the house. She wears protective goggles with dark lenses and a pair of Bose headphones she uses to keep her ears warm while listening to music on cold winter days. A colorful cashmere scarf is wrapped around the top of her brown Carhartt jacket to keep her neck warm.

Something about her touches Thomas. Suddenly, he's hit with a feeling he hasn't felt since the first moment he saw his wife in a white bathing suit walking along the edge of Shoshone Park's public swimming pool. He was 13 and she was 12. He was immediately captured by her, and he knew she was going to be a very important part of his life forever. He just knew it and so it happened, at least for a little while.

For 17 glorious years from the moment she said "I do", she was the reason he got up in the morning and came home at night. After a day full of tragedies, she was the one who sat beside him running her fingers through the hair on the back of his neck, and comforted him while they talked. She was the one who gave him a daughter to cherish. A daughter who left at the same time she did.

Now, that feeling is sweeping his soul again. It makes him want to shut down. *"I don't want to feel this!"* he silently screams to himself. He feels like running back down the alleyway, jumping back into the pickup truck, and high-tailing it to Shane's. It leaves him momentarily speechless.

Thomas' silence unnerves Kayla. She decides to step up and take the lead.

"Excuse me, Shelly Casey?" she calls out, but Shelly doesn't hear her over the music playing on the headphones and the intense concentration she has on what she's designing.

Kayla reaches out and taps her on the shoulder. Shelly almost knocks her sculpture over as she jumps up and pulls off her headphones.

"Who are you?" she rattles off, shocked by this sudden intrusion.

"I'm sorry, I didn't mean to scare you. I'm Detective Harrison, and this is Detective Shea, from Buffalo Homicide. Are you Mrs. Casey?"

A quizzical look crosses Shelly's face as the shock of being startled wears off.

"Umm, yes...I mean no. I used to be Mrs. Casey, but I've gone back to using my maiden name, Cortland", she slightly hunches her shoulders. "Divorced. "

Shelly looks at the both of them as she wonders why they are here.

"Did someone think I was dead?" Shelly asks.

"No, not you. Are you related to Theodore Casey?" Kayla asks.

Shelly switches back and forth, studying Kayla and Thomas' eyes looking to see if they are serious. Her eyes narrow as she realizes a long-held thought was now coming true.

"Teddy's dead?" she half asks, half says.

"I'm sorry," Kayla says in a sincere and soft way.

Shelly closes her eyes as she processes the information. This too strikes Thomas as being familiar as he reflects back on the knock on his screen door one beautiful spring evening as he was preparing to head out. He was on his way to attend what was left of his father's retirement party from the Buffalo police force at Conway Park after getting put of his work clothes.

Instead, he heard Detective Jim Wozniak yelling through the screen door. "Hey, Shea, you in here?"

Thomas stepped into the foyer and his eyes immediately connected with Wozniak's. He saw the pain in them and he knew right away his life had changed forever. Now, he's watching the same thing happen to someone else like he has done *so many Goddamn times before.*

Thomas watches Shelly's face as it changes from one emotion to another.

"What happened?" she asks.

Kayla isn't quite prepared to tell her as she glances downward.

Shelly shifts her gaze to Thomas.

"Is it that bad?" she asks him.

Thomas takes a deep breath before a long exhale.

"Someone really didn't like him," he responds.

"What do you mean?"

"Well, Mrs. Casey..."

She interrupts him. "It's not Mrs. Casey anymore. We divorced about seven months ago. Like I said, it's Shelly Cortland now...or again."

"Ms. Cortland, your husband was decapitated and his head and body were thrown into Lake Erie a few days ago," he says softly.

"Oh, my God. How do you know it was him?"

"We've been able to make a preliminary determination," Thomas replies.

Shelly leans back and closes her eyes to take it all in again. Her body heaves, but she fights back the tears that want to come out. Although she knows about hard living, she thought moments like these ended when Teddy came into her life and showed her a different way to live. He took her off the stage with a single pole where she danced for frustrated and creepy men, and some women, and learned about the worst in life from the best at making it bad. It made her learn what to expect when you should expect nothing.

In a moment, she clears her throat, opens her eyes, and looks deep into Thomas' eyes.

"I knew something bad would happen eventually," she whispers.

This strikes Thomas as odd.

"Why would that be?" he asks.

"Let me show you something," Shelly replies.

Shelly leads them over to a storage shed near the rear of the yard and opens the door to expose a partially completed marble statue. It's of a loving mother accepting a flower from the outstretched hand of a young child at her feet.

The statue knocks Thomas further back on his feet and he starts to fight back the tears drawing up in his eyes as he forces down the lump cramming his throat. He feels the need to run away even more quickly now to find a place to drown his emotions.

"He started this a little over four years ago. Seems like he worked on it day and night for a while. He really put his heart and soul into it, you know?" she reflects sadly as she glances into Thomas' eyes. "Then one day a couple of years ago, he came home and shut himself off from this...and from me."

Shelly shuts the door. "For some reason, he started running from life and it seemed like he never looked back."

She places her hand on the door, "I've always kept a little hope inside of me that he'd come back and finish it."

Thomas looks at Shelly.

"Do you know what made him change?"

I bet people are asking the same question about me, pops into his mind.

"I think, in the end, it was just a lot of things building up inside him that made him sad," Shelly replies. She leans forward and rests her head in sorrow against the wooden door. Her chest heaves a couple of times as she gulps in air to keep from breaking down.

Thomas feels the need to fold her up in his arms and absorb the pain she's experiencing, but he thinks it's probably wise if he didn't.

"I know this is hard, but can you come to do a positive identification of his remains for the medical examiner?" he asks.

"I thought you identified Teddy?" Shelly asks.

"We did, but we still need a relative to do a positive ID. Procedures," Thomas replies.

Shelly moves away from the door and takes another breath.

"I can do that," she says.

Thomas and Shelly look into each other's eyes more deeply this time. They see something most other people miss when they look into the same eyes. Something that reaches beyond the glance and goes to the soul. They see each other as they are, not as they seem.

"We'll drive you," Thomas says to her.

Shelly softens as she reacts to what she sees in his eyes.

"Thank you," she replies.

She takes off her glasses and earphones and sets them on the stool she was sitting on. She follows Thomas and Kayla out of the backyard, locking the gate behind her.

She moves a mess of takeout containers and cups to the side to make enough room to sit comfortably without getting anything on her.

"You seem to like takeout," Shelly says before she has a chance to catch herself.

Thomas meets her gaze by looking into the rear-view mirror.

"It's quick," he says to her.

Shelly looks at the debris scattered around her.

"So is throwing the mess in a garbage can."

Kayla bursts out a laugh. "Tell him. He doesn't listen to me."

Even Thomas has to laugh.

He and Shelly share another glance through the mirror; both seem thankful for the laugh in the midst of darkness.

Before long, they arrive at the entrance to the morgue located on the backside of the 12-story Erie County Medical Center. Thomas gets out and opens the door for Shelly. As she gets out, Thomas gently places his hand on the side of her arm.

"Have you ever done anything like this before?" he asks her.

Shelly sadly nods her head.

"It's been a long time, but yea," she replies.

He stares even more deeply into her eyes wondering why? She looks like she wants to tell him, but each knows now is not the time.

"Are you ready?" he finally asks.

Shelly nods her head again. "I think so."

"I'll be right beside you."

She feels his wounded soul as she looks at him gratefully. The feeling awakens emotions she has learned to suppress. Emotions she once loved having.

She finds it strange to suddenly feel attracted to someone right now. It makes her uncomfortable.

She steps away from Thomas a little bit.

"I think I'll be okay."

He drops his hand from her arm and leads her through the morgue's double-glass sliding doors into the reception area. They notice a long table off to the side. There's a wallet, keys, money, and a distinctive male wedding ring with elongated male and female figurines intertwined in a loving embrace sketched into the side of it. The items are placed neatly side-by-side.

Ozzie enters the room from the body storage area. He notices Shelly looking at the belongings laid out on the table. Like Thomas, there are things about his job he's grown to really hate and body identifications are at the top of the list just below the bodies of children getting wheeled in.

"Mrs. Casey?" Ozzie asks Shelly.

"It's Ms. Cortland now," Thomas chimes in.

"My apologies. I'm Dr. Osborne, Erie County Medical Examiner," Ozzie says to Shelly. "We have some things we'd like you to look at before we do the formal identification."

"Okay, she replies, her focus staying on the table."

Thomas drifts back to the moment when he rushed into the morgue and found Ozzie standing there crying. "Tommy" was all he said.

And Thomas instantly knew what Wozniak told him was true.
Ozzie motions to the table.

"Do these items look familiar do you?" Ozzie softly asks her.

"Oh, my God", Thomas remembers yelling as he looked at items sitting on the same table. He remembers instant fear and loneliness slamming through his soul. How he fell to his knees. How Ozzie held him to his chest while they wept.

She picks up the wedding ring and clutches it to her chest. Slowly, she starts to break down. Thomas' face tightens as he tries to hold back his emotions.

"Is this his ring?" Ozzie asks.

"Yes."

"Okay, just one more step."

Ozzie leads her to a small window with closed curtains in a wall in a private area of the viewing room.

"We've tried our best to make things look as good as possible. However, what we did clearly isn't enough. I'm sorry for that," Ozzie says sadly. "Are you ready?"

She nods her head, yes, but she's says quietly to herself, of course, I'm not ready. I don't even want to be here. I just want to be home and work on my sculpture.

Ozzie taps on the window. The curtain opens.

Teddy's body lays on a stainless steel table. The head has been positioned at the top of the body. A white sheet is used to cover the lower body and neck area to make the everything appear as natural as possible. Tears immediately flow from Shelly as she stumbles a little. Thomas reaches out and grabs her shoulders to steady her. She collapses in his chest. He hesitates at first but then folds her up in his arms.

Kayla's shocked by Thomas' sudden display of tenderness.

"Is this your husband?" Ozzie asks as gently as he can.

"Yes," she says while burying her face into Thomas' chest.

Thomas bends his head down and whispers into her ear.

"I know it's hard," he says.

She steps back a little and looks again into Thomas' eyes. She senses something.

"I think you do," she says softly.

"Thomas, we've got to get going," Kayla interrupts.

Thomas still stares into Shelly's eyes.

"We'll take you home first," he says to her.

"Actually, I would like to stay a little longer," she looks over at Ozzie. "Would it be okay if I stayed a little longer?"

"That is unusual," Ozzie replies. "This part of the hospital isn't set up for visitors."

"I promise to stay out of the way," she begs.

"Would you mind, Ozzie? I'd consider it a personal favor," Thomas interjects.

"Okay, we'll set you up an area to sit, but we don't really have any private areas where you can be alone," Ozzie explains.

Shelly sadly smiles. "That's okay."

She gives Thomas a big hug. "Thank you," she says to him.

Thomas lets her slip from his arms, even though he's never felt the need to keep on holding onto someone as badly as he does now.

Who am I kidding, he thinks,. *There's nothing here to love. I'm just a shell...with memories.*

He watches her walk away as Ozzie tries to find the nicest location for her to sit among the dead bodies and refrigerated storage units.

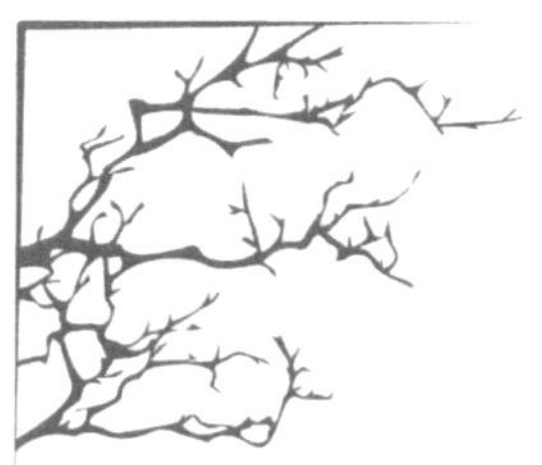

Chapter 13

Thomas finds himself sitting in his pickup near rotting black cast iron railings separating Broderick Park's parking lot from the strong currents of Niagara River. The darkness created by gray stormy clouds coming off the lake makes the midday hour seem like evening. Seagulls fly overhead before they dive down underneath the water's surface in search of something to eat for lunch.

He sits wondering about what exactly would happen that would get someone nasty enough to cut your head off. That takes someone who's on a mission. Someone who's making it personal.

Shelly did say her ex-husband changed over the years. Maybe he started hanging out with bad people. But of all the people Thomas has ever come across, meeting someone who cuts people's heads off isn't on the list. The people he knows are more likely to put a bullet in your head and dump your body in an alley than go through that type of effort.

No, this one is different. It's definitely personal. Whatever Theodore Casey did, his killer took exception to it and wanted Casey to really know how he felt. But what did he do? He picks up a pad and starts jotting down notes to keep his thoughts together.

Sunshine breaks through the clouds and lights up the river all the way over to the Canadian shoreline. It captures Thomas' attention. He sets the pad down and just looks at what he's watching. The beauty of it all.

He gets out of the pickup and walks over to the entrance of Bird Island Pier, which separates the Black Rock Canal from the swift waters running underneath the Peace Bridge and down to Niagara Falls. He reflects about on how he would come down here as a boy and walk the pier before they built it up to make it safer. Back then, when the tide came in, the water would rush over the rocks and he would get trapped on the pier until it dropped back down. Sometimes, he had to wait until late at night before he could get back to solid land.

Nowadays, there are flat concrete pads with wire railings to create a steady surface people can't easily fall off. A little disappointment settles inside Thomas as yet another memory of his past has changed. He walks out onto the pier.

His thoughts soon turn to Shelly. A little excitement digs through his dark soul to let him know new days could be possible - if he wanted it. He really liked how she felt in his arms and how her spirit said *life*.

The problem is he's not sure he wants to love anymore. Sometimes he feels he wants to go back to living and loving, and then other times, he just wants to be left alone. It makes for an uneasy existence, but he's getting used to it, or so he says to himself as he forces himself to think of something else.

Then his thoughts turn to his wife and daughter. How beautiful they were and how good they felt in his arms. How he would wake in the morning and just lay there staring at his sleeping bride. She would look so serene. He would sometimes wonder how life would be without her. The life he lived as a homicide detective always reinforced in him how quickly everything can change. People leaving in an instant was something he faced every day.

Then one day came, and he didn't have to wonder anymore.

He imagines the last thing she saw. How the tractor-trailer came right at them after the driver lost control. How it jumped the concrete barrier. How she steered the car onto the Louisiana Street exit ramp in a mad dash to get out of the truck's path. How it crashed into the car she was driving and his daughter was riding in.

And how, in an instant, they were both gone – along with his life.

He looks up at icicles hanging down from the Peace Bridge. They seem to be dripping tears on this warming winter day as the darkness descends back on his soul.

No, he says to himself, there's nothing left to love here.

And with that, he pushes everything out of his mind and heads back to his pickup to go to Shane's for a few.

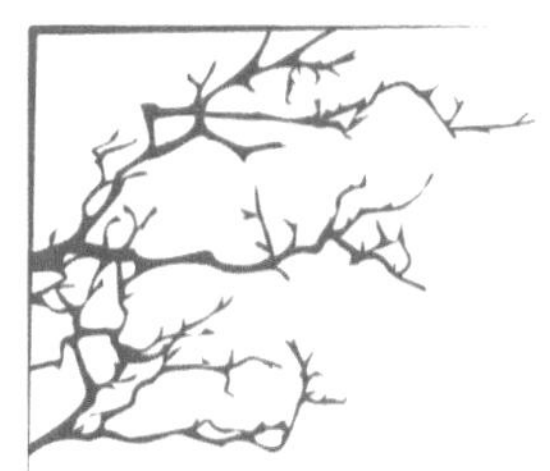

Chapter 14

From the top of Chestnut Ridge, the lights from downtown Buffalo brighten up the distant night sky. The toboggan and sledding hills are closed and all the families and friends have loaded into their cars and headed home. Heavy winds blowing off of Lake Erie bends the trees along the edge of the parking lot.

Troy sees a Subaru Outback remaining in the lot as he drives a small dump truck from one garbage can to another to empty them. He fihures it's probably young lovers still hiking on one of the many trails in the surrounding woods, and he figures he'll keep an eye on it to make sure they get back and leave before he's done for the night. If he has to, he'll call the sheriff to look for them to make sure they are alright.

He drives over to the lodge and stops in a dark area where the trash containers are kept behind a wooden-gated area. As he gets out of the truck wearing his green maintenance winter suit, he notices a light on in the lodge through a window.

Troy walks to a side door and lets himself in to find Debbie struggling to reach the shutoff switch for the fans on the hood over the grills.

"Hi, Debbie, you need some help?" Troy asks her.

Debbie jumps up a little bit as she quickly turns around.

"Mr. Englewood, you scared me!"

"I'm sorry about that," he replies. "Do you need help?"

"Sure," she steps away from the grill. "Would you mind turning off the fans? Bobby usually does it before he leaves, but I guess he forgot and the grills are still too hot for me to lean over them."

A warm smile crosses Troy's face.

"I sure can," he replies. He walks over and easily reaches the switch with his long arm.

A slightly embarrassed and hesitant look appears on Debbie's face.

"Um, how's Jeff?" she asks.

A surprised look comes over Troy.

"He hasn't been over?"

"No."

Troy shakes his head and chuckles a little bit.

"Well, he will be. Trust me."

A hopeful look comes over Debbie.

"Really?" she replies as she looks at the gray hair lining Troy's handsome face. She wonders if Jeff is going to look like him when he gets older. She hopes he does.

"I know so," he says with a great big smile. "Need anything else?"

"Thank you, but I've just got a little more to clean up, and then I'll be going home."

"Okay, well, I've got to finish up taking out the trash. If you need me, I'll be outside somewhere."

"Thanks again, Mr. Englewood." Then Debbie remembers the man from yesterday. "Oh, one more thing, a man came by yesterday looking for you. He said he was an old friend."

"Really? Did he leave a name?"

"No. he just said he'd stop back today sometime, but I haven't seen him."

"What does he look like?" Troy asks.

"Umm, kind of regular. He had on a stupid-looking beard."

Troy smiles.

"A stupid-looking beard?"

"Yea, I don't know. Just looked funny."

"Okay, well, thank you."

Debbie motions to the hood over the grill.

"Thank you, again, too!"

"You're welcome," Troy replies as he leaves.

Outside, Troy walks inside the wooden fenced-in area where the trash cans are kept.

He hears a voice.

"I've been waiting for you," it says.

Troy turns to find Brian standing right behind him. Before he can do anything, Brian lunges a syringe into the side of his neck. In moments, he feels sluggish and drops to the ground. He's unable to move or make a sound. The only thing that lets Brian know Troy is alive is the startled look in his eyes and his faint breathing.

Moving and placing Troy into the back of the maintenance pickup truck takes more effort than Brian realized it would, but, eventually, he's able to load him into the back for the short ride over to the maintenance shed.

He parks the truck in a dark place around the side of the maintenance shed where he can keep an eye out on the lodge. Soon, Debbie walks out and gets into her little hatchback and drives away. Brian gets out of the truck and walks around back to grab the ring of keys hanging from Troy's belt. He gets into the garage and raises the main door.

Then he circles back and gets into the truck. He drives it around the front and backs it in through the garage door until he reaches a wood chipper. Brian climbs into the back and loads Troy into the chipper feet first.

He stares into Troy's horror-filled eyes.

"You should have listened," Brian says as he starts the machine.

The blades in the chipper start spinning around. Brian climbs up on the back of the pickup and lifts up Troy's limp body. He pushes the body to the edge of the chipper and sticks Troy's feet over it. Then he pushes down on Troy's shoulder until the blades grab Troy's feet and legs and start grinding them up. Flesh, bone, and blood splatter all over the equipment and vehicles inside the maintenance garage.

Suddenly, the chipper stops as the blades start grinding his hip bones and lower abdomen.

Brian gets down from the pickup and goes over to the chipper. He looks inside it to make sure nothing is stuck that would have activated the emergency shutoff switch but he doesn't see anything. Then he looks at the fuel gauge. It's empty. He looks back into Troy's eyes as his life fades away. No need for more, he thinks, just be a waste of gas.

He closes the garage door behind him and walks into the growing winds.

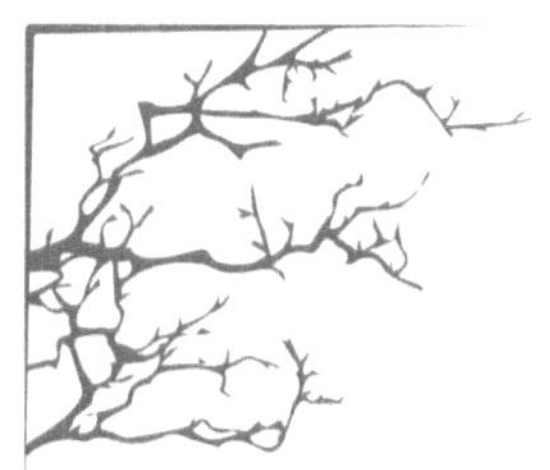

Chapter 15

The soft light from a table lamp on the nightstand next to Father Isaiah's bed shines down on the book he is reading. The sound of tires crunching over snow in the parking area outside his window grabs his attention. He sets the book down on his chest and listens.

The car soon comes to a stop and Isaiah hears a door shut. Then, he hears the crunching of footsteps in the snow as someone passes under his window. Moments later, he hears the kitchen door open and shut beneath his bedroom floor.

Father Isaiah sets his book on his bed, gets up, puts on a gray linen bathrobe, and steps out into the hallway. He makes his way to the oak staircase leading to the first floor.

Brian hears Father Isaiah get up and walk across his bedroom floor. He stops to listen as the footsteps move out into the hallway and head toward the stairs. He quickly searches around for something, anything, to make it look like everything's normal.

Father Isaiah reaches the landing on the first floor and tip-toes over to the kitchen door. He pushes it open enough to see Brian making a ham and cheese sandwich.

"Would you like a sandwich?" Brian calls out.

Pushing the door wide open, Father Isaiah enters the small commercial-like kitchen with stainless steel pots hanging from a rack over the stove and walnut cabinets with little glass windows along one wall.

"Out late again?" Father Isaiah asks.

Brian looks at Father Isaiah's reflection in the window over the counter. He knows he has to be careful.

"I had to meet someone," Brian replies.

"At this time of night?"

"Sometimes you have to meet people when they can. Sure you don't want a sandwich?"

Father Isaiah shakes his head no. He watches Brian pour a glass of milk and heads out into the dining room. Father Isaiah follows him.

Brian sits at the large oak table in the ornate dining room. A colorful Tiffany chandelier hangs down over the table. Father Isaiah takes a seat in a high-back cushioned chair at the other end of the table. He watches as Brian starts to eat his sandwich.

"Did you not hear me calling to you in the hallway the other night?"

"No," Brian says matter-of-factually.

"I also knocked on your bedroom door right after you entered it."

"Did you knock hard?" Brian asks.

"No, it was a soft rap. Why do you ask?"

"I had my earphones in. That's probably why I didn't hear you," Brian responds.

Father Isaiah's eyes narrow as he studies Brian.

"You seemed...disheveled. Like something was wrong."

"I saw something that really upset me."

Father Isaiah patiently waits for Brian to continue for a few moments before becoming a little impatient.

"Do you want to continue? he asks.

"Actually, it wasn't what I saw that bothered me. I was dealing with some flashbacks from my younger days. Things I don't want to remember. That's why I was out. I had to go for a walk to get over the images," Brian responds.

Brian studies Father Isaiah as much as Father Isaiah is studying him. Brian is checking to see if Father Isaiah looks like he's believing him. The deceit is starting to feel good as Father Isaiah's eyes soften and he appears sympathetic.

"The whole thing just shook me up," Brian continues. "I was a little out of sorts until I got some exercise and rest."

"I'm sorry. I know bad things happened to you."

A moment of silence falls over the table.

"You know, you can always talk to me when the memories get bad?" Father Isaiah says.

"I do."

"Well, I'm going back to bed. You'll clean up and turn off the lights before heading to bed?"

Brian nods yes.

Isaiah walks away still feeling a little disconcerted by the way Brian acted the other night, but he's just not sure. He feels strongly that Brian might be up to something and he hopes it's not something that could embarrass the diocese. He's grown to be very protective about the church in ways he never thought he would after so many priests were accused of molesting children. He hopes Brian isn't following in their path.

Brian bites into his sandwich as he watches Father Isaiah disappear down the hallway. His thoughts turn to a certain nurse. A nurse who also wouldn't listen to him.

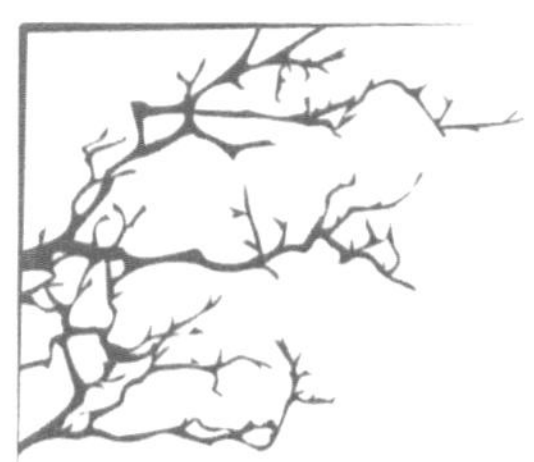

Chapter 16

Sun shines on the packed snow on the sledding hill at Chestnut Ridge Park. Kids of all ages fly down the steep hillside on their sleds and toboggans. A green utility van with "Erie County Parks Department" stenciled on the side doors comes up the road and stops at the rustic lodge at the top of the hill.

Jeff Englewood, a young man with an athletic build, jumps out of the van and glides past merry sledders into the rustic lodge with a roaring fire going in the big red-stoned fireplace. He looks at the kids running around as families eat packed and bought lunches at long communal tables lined up and down the cavernous room.

Jeff quickly moves through the crowd and heads to the front of the concession area. Debbie's bright eyes shine when she spots him as she hands a kid a slice of pizza.

He takes Debbie all in as he waits behind two restless kids who are pushing and shoving each other. They both grab their slices of pizza and head off to another area of the building.

Jeff steps up to the counter.

A shy smile crosses Debbie's face.

"Hi, Jeff."

"Hey, Debbie."

"What are you doing here?"

"I came to pick up the wood chipper. A couple of trees tipped over in the wind last night on the other side of the park."

Debbie tilts her head a little.

"Where's your dad? Doesn't he usually handle that?"

"Don't know. He probably went to Kate's to play cards upstairs, got drunk, and slept in since he usually doesn't start until later in the day. The problem is a tree is blocking a road and needs to be removed and they weren't able to get him. So, they sent me up here to get a couple of chainsaws and the wood chipper."

Debbie coyly looks up at Jeff.

"Want a hot chocolate?"

Jeff flashes her a big smile.

"Sure."

The hot chocolate machine whirls as Debbie presses the button to release the steamy chocolate mixture into a thick paper cup. A dreamy look crosses Jeff's face as he watches her.

Debbie raises her voice over the sound of the machine.

"He was here last night when I closed."

Jeff's lost in his thoughts of lust and love.

"Who," he asks.

"Your dad," she says as she rolls her eyes at him. "He helped me close up last night".

"That was nice," Jeff responds.

"Your dad's a nice man."

She hands him his hot chocolate.

"Here you go."

Jeff reaches into his pocket for money. Debbie waves her hand.

"On the house."

Jeff's eyes brighten. "Thanks!"

"Let me know when you reach your dad."

"Yea, I will."

Jeff floats on a cloud as he leaves and gets back into his van. He notices the back corner of his dad's car parked around the corner of the maintenance garage as he pulls away from the lodge.

Jeff drives up the hill toward the garage and pulls up next to his dad's Ford Explorer.

He bounces out of the van and rushes into the garage.

"Hey, dad, they finally got a hold of you!" he yells out just before he notices what's in the chipper.

As Thomas drives past the now nearly deserted sledding area. He gets directed by a police officer to head toward the maintenance garage where most of the sledders have gathered to watch what is going on.

Directly parked outside the garage is about a dozen police cars and an ambulance crew sitting idling.

As Thomas pulls to a stop, he watches as a police officer rushes out the garage door and pukes alongside the building. He then notices Kayla pulling up behind him. Thomas gets out and meets her after she parks.

Officer Lucas Jamison, a grizzled veteran of the streets, stops Thomas and Kayla as they make their way to the garage.

Thomas looks at him.

"Lucas, you don't look so good."

"This is about the worst I've seen. Prepare yourself."

"It can't be that bad."

"Trust me on this."

Thomas notices Debbie holding Jeff as he rocks back and forth on a bench. He motions to them.

"Who are they?"

"That's the victim's son, Jeff. He found his dad," Lucas looks at his notes, "A Troy Englewood about an hour ago. She's a friend, her name's Debbie. From what we know, she was the last person to see the victim alive...except for the killer, that is," Lucas responds.

"You think she could have done it?" Kayla asks.

Lucas looks at Debbie's small frame. "Not a chance."

Thomas looks over at Kayla.

"Shall we go in?" he asks.

"I guess we better," she says, devoid of enthusiasm. Thomas notices and smiles a little bit. Looks like she's becoming a homicide detective rather quickly.

"Let's go, then."

Kayla grimaces as Lucas steps to the side.

"It's all yours," he says as Thomas and Kayla head into the garage.

A crime scene photographer is busy taking photos of the body.

"Jesus, what is it with people this week?" Thomas says. Kayla instantly feels like she's going to puke as she looks at the blood, tissue, and bone sprayed all over the inside of the maintenance garage. She heaves when she notices Troy's upper torso resting in the hopper. His wide and dead eyes stare right at her.

She fights the urge to run out.

Thomas steps up close to the chipper to get a closer look.

The puke water flooding Kayla's mouth slowly subsides as she battles back the urge to get sick. Finally, feeling somewhat composed, she starts examining marks on the floor.

"Looks like he was brought in a car or truck and dumped," she says.

Thomas glances down at the floor and nods in agreement.

Kayla leans closer to marks along the dirty floor.

"We've got shoe prints," she adds.

Thomas motions over to the photographer. "Hey, have you taken photos of the floor?"

"Not yet."

"Take some over here, before the rest of the circus arrives. Will ya?"

"Can do."

The photographer walks over to the area Thomas points to and starts taking shots of the floor. Thomas and Kayla go back outside to give him room to work.

Thomas watches as Josh, the crusty reporter who waved at him in the bar, busily writes things down on a notepad as he walks next to Dr. Ozzie.

Thomas stops them both.

"Hey, Oz, before you go in, we're taking pictures before more things get disturbed. It'll take a minute.

Josh looks at Thomas. "You gotta lead?"

"Don't know."

Ozzie looks at Thomas impatiently, "I've got to pronounce him dead and get back to the office, Tommy. Things to do and people to meet sort of thing."

"Trust me, he's dead. It'll only take a few minutes."

The look on Thomas' face softens. "How'd she do, Doc?"

Ozzie at first wonders who he's talking about.

"Mrs. Casey?" he asks.

"It's Ms. Cortland now," Thomas replies.

"Nice lady," Josh adds.

"You've met her?" Thomas asks Josh.

"Interviewed her actually. Doc said her husband was alive and conscious when he," Josh moves his index finger across his throat, "got it"

Ozzie interjects, "I only mentioned it was a possibility. And that was in confidence."

Thomas looks back at Josh. "Did you mention that to her?

"No, she left before Doc figured it out."

The photographer walks out of the maintenance garage and gives Thomas a thumbs-up.

Thomas motions to Ozzie.

"Okay, Oz, you're free to go in."

Josh starts to follow Ozzie, but Thomas grabs his arm.

"You stay here."

"Hey, man, freedom of the press," Josh protests.

"Not now."

Josh watches Ozzie walk inside the garage.

"How bad is it?" Josh asks.

"Bad."

They grow silent for a moment. then Thomas then leans over to whisper into Josh's ear.

"Hey, do me a favor?"

"What's that?"

"Keep the information about Casey being alive and aware when he died quiet for now."

"It's part of the story, Thomas."

"I know. Just a day or two."

"Why?"

"Consider it a personal favor."

Josh studies Thomas, he's not used to him asking any type of favor in all the years he's known him. He senses the seriousness.

"I can't promise anything, but I'll see what I can do. You know the editors have the final say on things and I've already submitted the article."

"I do. But if you could find a way to hold off, I'd appreciate it."

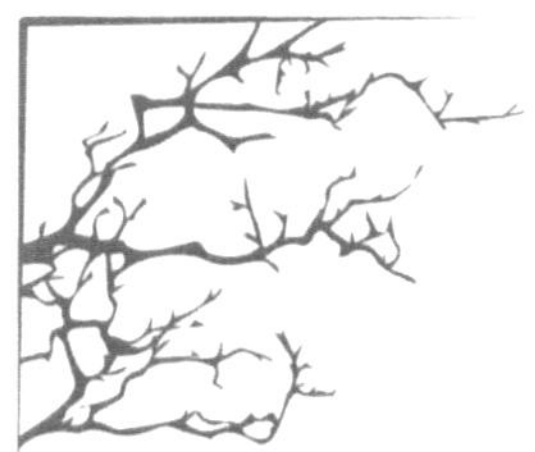

Chapter 17

Thomas sits at his desk in police headquarters as he stares out the window at the falling snow filling the void between him and St. Joseph's Old Cathedral. He pulls a fresh pint of Old Granddad out of his jacket pocket and takes a long hard swig.

Kayla comes in carrying a file. She gives a disapproving glance when she notices the bottle. Thomas quickly puts it away.

"We got the analysis back on the shoe print casts you took in front of the grain elevator," she says to him.

"That was quick."

"Pretty serious case with all the media attention."

She hands him the file.

"The shoe type belongs to a non-slip Hardy shoe. You know, the kind beat cops wear," she adds.

"That doesn't mean anything. A lot of people wear those types of shoes. They're easy to take care of and great for winter walking." Thomas nods toward the church. "I've even seen priests and restaurant workers wear the same shoe."

"So, in other words, the cast means nothing?"

"Not necessarily," Thomas says as he looks at the cast images. "We now know one thing for certain: it's a man's shoe style, size 10. That means we are looking for someone who is probably five foot six to five foot nine inches tall. Also, look here, you see how the side of the right shoe is worn down more than the rest of the shoe?"

Kayla studies the image.

"Yea, I see it."

"The perp suffers from underpronation."

"What's that?" Kayla asks.

"It's caused when a person's foot doesn't roll over to absorb the impact of walking. Instead, the weight of the foot just presses down on the outer edge of the shoe, causing it to wear down faster than the rest of the shoe. It's an identifier we'll use to match up any shoes we find."

"Interesting," Kayla says.

"There's a lot to learn from a shoe print."

"I guess so," she beams a wide smile at him.

"Has the photographer made images of the prints at Chestnut Ridge?" Thomas asks.

"He got called to a couple of other situations and won't get to it until the morning."

Thomas leans back in his chair, stretches his arms, and yawns.

"I'm ready to call it a day," he says as he snaps himself forward and rises from the chair.

"Where you headed?" Kayla asks.

"Might go to the center to sit or I might go home. I don't know."

"You going to be okay?"

A soft smile crosses his face as she looks into his doubtful eyes.

"That does seem to be the question with you, isn't it?" he says.

"Call me an old hen."

"You're too young to be an old hen and you're too new to be worrying about me. I've been around forever now and I'll be around when forever's done."

"I just want you to know..."

Thomas cuts her off before she finishes. "Seriously, let it go for tonight. Okay?"

"Yea, sure."

"Thanks. I'll see you tomorrow."

"Yea."

"Great."

Thomas grabs his coat and heads out.

Thomas exits the side door of police headquarters. He turns toward the back parking lot and walks directly into the wind. The cold bites at the exposed skin on his face.

The stone walls of the cathedral catches his attention as he turns into the back parking lot.

He stares up at the steeple as gray clouds release their barrage of snow down onto the earth. A strange feeling comes over him that makes him feel compelled to enter.

The memories come swooping back to him as he steps inside the foyer. He hasn't stood in this spot since he was a boy when he came here with his Uncle Joe.

Walking into the cavernous cathedral makes him feel like he is stepping back in time. He takes each step slowly, trying to be careful in case the memories rush to him too fast. It's like he can almost hear the voices of years gone by; the silent murmurings, slight coughs, and whispered admonishments to slightly overactive children as the priest gave his sermon. The thoughts lighten his heart as he takes a seat in one of the long wooden pews.

He looks up near the altar at the section he used to sit with his uncle. He can see himself as a boy as he remembers how his uncle would hand him a dollar to put in the basket the ushers would carry as they walked down the aisle. The ushers would stop at each row and stretch the woven reed basket with a burgundy liner across the pew with its long handle. As it passed by him, he'd reach up and put the dollar his Uncle Joe gave him into it.

The memories relax him.

He takes little notice of Brian as he replaces the candles on the altar, but Brian has taken notice of him. Brian recognizes him as one of the officers he sees coming in and out of the police headquarters almost daily. But, he knows he's never seen Thomas in here before; he wonders why he has such a solemn look on his face. What could be torturing his soul?

He decides to step off the altar and approach Thomas to ask.

He sets the last of the candles into the holders before he turns around to approach Thomas, but when he turns, he sees Thomas slipping out the front doors.

Later, as Brian watches the news on TV, a story comes on about the killing at Chestnut Ridge. As cameras pan over the maintenance garage, he spots Thomas standing at the front of it as he talks to a couple of other cops. He can tell by how they are reacting to him that he's one of the people in charge.

Brian starts wondering again. He looks up at the heavens. Is this a sign showing me who I should help, he thinks? Who is this man who grabbed his attention on this wintry night?

He wants to know, and he intends to find out – if they ever meet again.

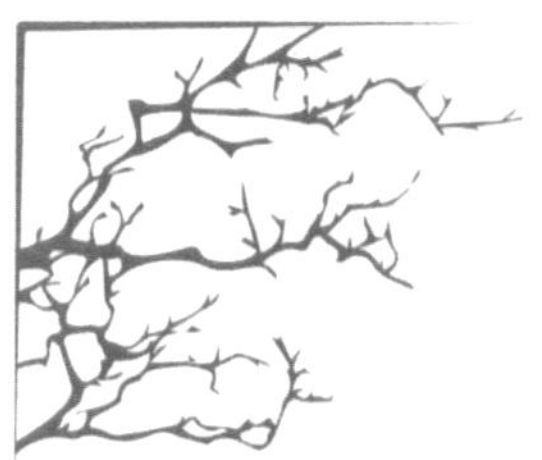

Chapter 18

The dim light of morning filters in the window at the end of the hallway of Thomas' apartment building as the newspaper boy, actually an older man - they stopped using kids years ago because of the fear of grabbers and pedophiles - drops the morning edition of the Buffalo Courier Express at each door as he makes his way along the corridor.

The paper plops down at Thomas' doorstep. The headline screams *MAN ALIVE AND ALERT WHEN BEHEADED.*

Inside Thomas' bedroom, he groggily flips over to shut off a ringing alarm clock.

He sets the picture of his wife and daughter on the nightstand as he gets up and sits on the edge of the bed, ready to face another wonderful day. Actually, he feels pretty good, he didn't drink last night, and being in the cathedral lifted up his spirits a little; just like it did when he was a boy with his Uncle Joe.

Dressed in boxers and a T-shirt, Thomas stumbles out of the bedroom and into the kitchen, where he gets his bottle of Old Granddad out of the cupboard.

He pours himself one, raises the glass in a toast toward the ray of sunshine coming through the window, and slugs it back. If anything, he's a man of habit.

Then, he looks in the refrigerator. It's as bleak as the Arctic tundra on a cold day. He pours another quick one and shoots it down. He walks across the living room and opens the front door to grab the newspaper.

The headline stops him in his tracks, and a fire begins to burn in his eyes.

He crosses over to "12A" and bangs on the door. Repeatedly.

Josh opens the door. Thomas shoves the paper in his face.

"What's this?" he shouts.

Josh wipes the sleep from his eyes before he can focus on the headline. A huge smile grows on his face as his eyes sparkle.

"I got the headline!"

"Screw the headline. What the hell are you doing putting this in the paper?"

"It's news."

"You promised."

"I promised I'd try. The editor said no. We had to run with it."

"Jesus, have you thought about how Ms. Cortland's going to feel when she sees this?"

"Hey, I didn't kill her husband. I only reported what happened."

Thomas' face turns red with anger.

"Josh, sometimes you just piss me off."

"Oh, and you don't piss people off?" Josh shoots back.

"Crap. I'm just wasting my time. Go back to bed."

Thomas stomps back across the hall and slams the door shut behind him as he re-enters his apartment.

Thomas sits with the paper on his lap and his bottle of old granddad in his hand; he tips the bottle back and takes a huge slug. The good feelings from the night before wash away with each slug he takes.

The drunken gaze of determination fills Thomas' eyes.

He gets up, dresses, and leaves the apartment.

Thomas pulls up in front of Shelly's artistic home and parks where he can see into the backyard. He notices the shed's door is open. Within a moment or two, he sees the top of Shelly's head as she walks in and out of the shed.

Raising his small flask to his lips, he takes a swig as he debates getting out of the pickup truck and walking into the backyard. There's a stirring in him he can't ignore even though he knows he's in no shape to be paying attention to it, but she creates an urge in him that cries to be filled.

The thinking requires another swig.

He finally comes to a decision: he should drive on. He knows he should. He thinks he should while he opens the door to his pickup and gets out. He thinks it as he walks across the street and up the shoveled walkway to the gate that leads into the backyard. He still thinks it as he opens the gate and steps into the backyard.

He stops thinking it as soon as he lays his eyes on Shelly.

She sits on a bucket and stares at the unfinished sculpture, tears streaming from her eyes. The newspaper lies on the ground next to her; the headline faces upward.

Thomas comes up behind her.

"I'm sorry," he says softly.

Startled, Shelly jumps up.

"Oh, my God, I didn't even hear you come in! What is it with you people?" she gasps.

"Yea, sorry about that, too. I saw the paper this morning and, I don't know, I wanted to see how you were."

The sincerity in Thomas' eyes touches something again in Shelly. She starts to wonder if she should start thinking about this man showing her so much concern. She feels she could, but she also feels it'd be a dangerous thing to do. She's not sure if she's ready to try or even if she wants to.

"How could someone be so cruel?" she asks him.

"I'm not sure," he replies, wishing he had a better answer. But he doesn't and, at this point in his life, he's not sure if he ever will.

His face softens even more.

"You okay?" he asks Shelly.

Shelly sits back down with a sort of defeated slump in her shoulders.

"I don't know. You spend so much of your life hoping and dreaming for other people, and then when what you hope and dream for doesn't happen..." She says before she looks up into Thomas' hazel eyes. "You can bear it better when there's still a chance."

"What was he like?" Thomas asks.

"He used to be very kind. Always had a twinkle in his eyes and a constant laugh. God, he could make me laugh even on the darkest days."

"You said he changed before. How?"

"It started slowly at first, but then one day he came home and the Teddy I had always known and loved was no longer there," she says with reflective sadness.

"What happened?"

"I don't really know. Working in a prison didn't agree with him over time, I suppose. He thought he was going to be able to open new worlds for the women imprisoned with his art. It seemed he lost faith in his abilities one day, and he could never get it back. He just slipped into a dark world and shut the door behind him. He never told me if something happened, and if something did, whatever it was, they kept it hush-hush."

Thomas leans in close to take her hand.

"Again, I'm so sorry for your pain."

She sniffs the air as he speaks.

"Have you been drinking?" she asks.

"What?"

"It's nine-thirty in the morning!"

Thomas stands back up, feeling like he just got gut-punched.

"I...um," he stammers.

"How do you expect to find his killer drunk?" she demands.

"I'm sorry, Ms. Cortland. I try my best," he says with a slight defensiveness in his voice.

"So far, your best isn't impressive."

"I manage," he says as he starts to grit his teeth a little.

"Do you?"

"Yea, I do."

"Well, good luck, Detective Shea. Tell me something, does your partner start drinking this early, too?"

Thomas closes his eyes for a moment to collect himself and control his rising anger.

Finally, he says, "I know you're angry…"

"You have no idea!" She cuts him off. "Can I be left alone now?"

Thomas just looks at her for a moment, He realizes he's screwed up by drinking and coming here. All he was trying to do was show he cared, but now, he knew it was time to slink away.

He slowly walks toward the gate before slowly turning around.

"I just wanted to help," he says almost sheepishly.

"You've done a fine job. Be happy," Shelly snaps.

Thomas looks hurt. "I…"

Shelly cuts him off again. "Goodbye, Detective."

Thomas opens the gate and walks out.

Climbing back into his truck, he grabs the flask of Old Granddad out of his pocket and uncaps it. Puts it to his lips but stops before the liquid gold enters his throat.

He stares at it with contempt, trying to remember when the damn stuff started taking over his life.

Looking into his rear-view mirror back at himself he thinks he knows when it started; actually, he knows exactly when it started happening.

He glances over at the top of Shelly's head as she closes the shed door.

Thomas recaps the bottle, starts the pickup, and drives away.

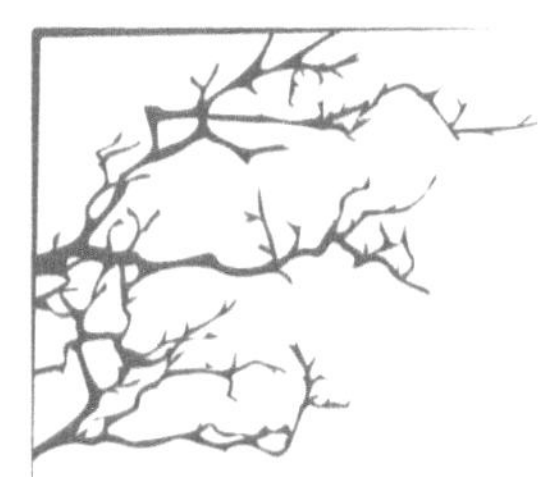

Chapter 19

The extravagance of the Bishop's office surrounds Father Isaiah as he sits in a Victorian-styled wooden high-back chair with red velvet-covered cushions. The only sound in the room is coming from the handmade Austrian-Vienna wall clock.

The thudding echo of flat shoes walking across a carpeted floor grabs his attention as he looks down the hallway. A modestly dressed older woman with a pair of dark-rimmed eyeglasses hanging around her neck with a silver chain walks briskly toward him.

"Father Isaiah, the Bishop will see you now. Please come with me," she says.

Isaiah rises and follows her down the hallway. She leads him through heavy oak doors into an opulent office. The rotund Bishop, dressed in a black robe with amaranth and purple fascia trim, a gold pectoral cross hanging over his chest, and a purple-colored amethyst ecclesiastical ring on his finger, rises from his large maple wood executive desk and comes around to greet Isaiah.

"Father, it's so good to see you," he says as he claps both hands around Isaiah's extending right hand. "It's been too long since we've sat and talked."

"I know you're busy, Your Excellency, but I'm afraid I've come to express concerns about the young man living at the Cathedral."

"The one considering the priesthood?" the Bishop asks.

"Yes," Father Isaiah feels a little hesitant because he's still not sure what he's exactly concerned about.

"May I sit down," he asks the Bishop.

The Bishop nods and extends his hand toward another high-back wooden chair with velvet-covered cushions. He takes a seat in an identical chair next to Isaiah's.

"Please, Isaiah, what bothers you?"

"You know, Clarence... Oh, I'm, sorry, your excellency," Isaiah catches himself.

The Bishop chuckles a little and leans in toward Isaiah. "Isaiah, we've been friends since before we put on these robes. What is it, and forget the formalities."

Father Isaiah smiles briefly before his face turns grave again.

"I think that young man staying at the Cathedral is going to take us further into the darkness we've been working so hard to leave."

"You think he's been having relations with minors?" the Bishop asks bluntly.

"I don't know, but he's doing something that gives me worry, and he needs to be carefully monitored."

"Well, monitoring him is your job. That's why we assigned him to you."

"I know," Father Isaiah responds, "but I can't be the only one who knows when I have suspicions. That's where your ability to monitor me comes in."

The Bishop sits back in his chair.

"True," he says. "What do you think he's doing?"

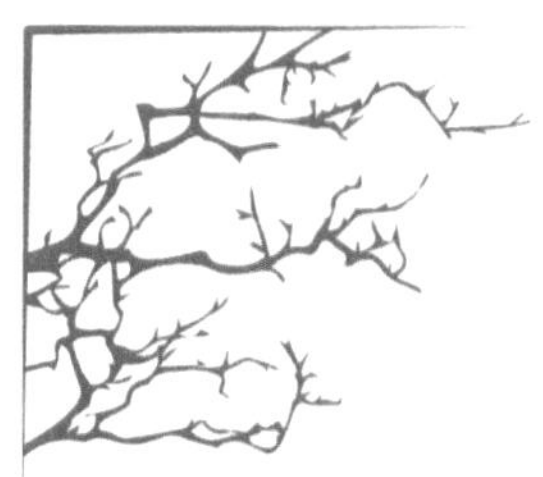

Chapter 20

Thomas drives around, his mind in a fog. He drives onto the Niagara Thruway and heads along the river toward Niagara Falls. He feels he just lost his chance. Like something he would have liked could have happened.

Like something he really missed about feeling alive.

He finds himself at the entrance to Mt. Olivet Cemetery near the exit he uses to get off the thruway. He turns into the cemetery and snakes himself around to the back part, and parks in front of two rows of well-trimmed arborvitae trees lining each side of a pathway leading to the Sacred Heart of Mary Shine set in the back.

His right hand trembles as he reaches for his bottle. It takes all he has to put it back in his pocket as he opens his pickup truck's door. He walks up the snow-covered grass lawn until he reaches the sixth tree on his left side.

The tree his wife and child are buried under.

He falls to his knees and brushes the snow away from the flattened headstone half buried in the ground. Their names appear. He slumps his shoulders and starts rocking back and forth as tears flow from his eyes.

He wants them back so badly. Just for them to be alive for one more moment, so he can gather them up in his loving arms. In his memories, he can smell their hair and the perfume his daughter wore because mommy wore it. He remembers how they danced and laughed while listening to the music of today and the past. Life was grand then.

Grander than he ever realized at the time.

His hand touches the bottle before he pulls it away again.

The day seems warm to him. Like the really chilly cold has subsided for a few hours. He feels tired. Worn to the bone.

He lays down over the graves and rests his head against his gloved hands. Within seconds, the alcohol-induced tiredness of his morning drinking has him sound asleep.

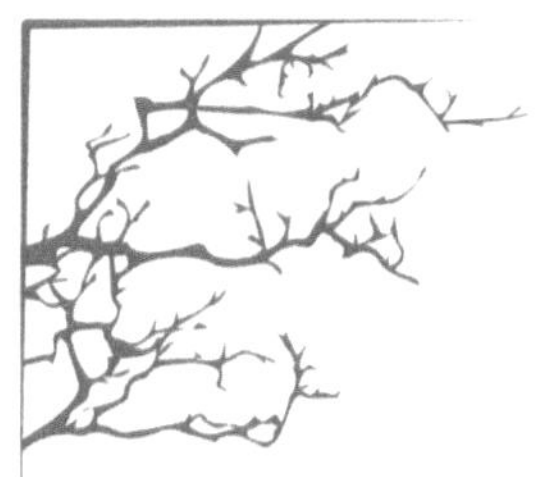

Chapter 21

Answering the door brought more questions than answers to Shelly, like *why is this young woman standing in my doorway?*

"Ms. Cortland, I'm Detective Harrison, we met the other day," Kayla says.

Shelly looks at her. She remembers.

"Your partner was already here this morning," she says flatly.

"He was?"

"Yea, and he was drunk."

Kayla seems confused, "I'm sorry, but when was this?"

"A couple of hours ago."

"A couple of hours...," Kayla says as she wonders where he is now.

"C'mon in," Shelly says as she relents and steps away from the door.

Kayla steps in and looks around. She instantly feels like she's entered an enchanted land of wonderment. There are paintings and sculptures everywhere of mystical mountains, exploding solar events, windy forests, and other places the mind likes to go when wandering.

"I hope you don't mind. I'd like to ask a few more questions," Kayla says.

"Actually, I have a few questions myself."

"You do?" Kayla squints her eyelids.

"I do," Shelly replies, "But you first."

Kayla asks her what she already knew. There was nothing new to add, and Kayla felt comfortable that all of the bases were totally covered. Then Shelly looks straight into her eyes.

"What happened to your partner?" she asks.

"What do you mean?" Kayla says as alarm bells go off in her head.

"You know what I mean," Shelly responded. "Why is he trying to kill himself?"

"I'm not sure I know what you're talking about."

"You know, Detective. There's a pain in that man's eyes as well as a...gentleness. What's causing that pain?"

In some ways, Kayla's been waiting for the moment someone was going to ask her that question. A question she's been trying to answer herself. A question that's not allowed to be talked about in police headquarters, but one she really wants to talk about. Not because she wants to gossip, but because it helps her sort things out that she doesn't quite understand. And what Thomas is going through is something she is really trying to understand.

"Sit down," Kayla says as she grabs a seat at the dining table and sits down herself. "He's, uh, been through a lot," she says, "His wife and daughter were headed to an evening softball game between Buffalo Police and Fire. They, uh, didn't make it."

"What happened?" Shelly asks.

"They were getting off the Louisiana Street exit on the Thruway when a tractor-trailer lost control and crashed into them."

The thought of what happened brings tears to Kayla's eyes as she struggles to swallow.

"The car burst into flames," she continues, "People heard them screaming but the fire was quicker than those trying to help. They couldn't get them out. They burned alive. The paper reported his daughter just kept screaming out for her daddy until..." Kayla bites her lip to hold back the emotion. The realization of what Thomas must feel on a daily basis seeped into her soul as she spoke. The horror he must feel hits her hard.

"Oh, my God," Shelly whispers softly.

Kayla struggles to continue. "Shortly after the accident, his mother was diagnosed with Alzheimer's Disease. She's been hospitalized for about six months now. Thomas spends a lot of time sitting by her side as he watches her fade away."

"I get it," Shelly says as she reflects on the time when she was someone different - before she became who she is now.

"I understand, too, but somehow, someway, he's got to come to terms with what happened and what he has to do to gain control over his life again, or he's going to completely lose everything. There's been talk around," Kayla says with a hint of desperation.

"How do you think you'll be able to convince him of that?" Shelly asks.

"I don't know," Kayla responds.

Shelly's soft but knowing eyes lock with Kayla's tearful ones.

"You know, nothing's going to happen until he wants to change."

"I know."

Kayla feels she's said more than enough and rises. She shakes Shelly's hand.

"Do me a favor, don't let it slip we talked about him like this. He wouldn't like it," she asks.

Shelly rises. "I promise," she says.

Kayla walks to the front door. She turns as she opens the door.

"Thank you, Ms. Cortland."

"For what?"

"For listening, talking about Thomas is a serious 'no-no' down at the station. Especially for us younger members."

"You're welcome, Detective Harrison. I'm glad he has a partner that cares about him as much as it seems you do."

"Yea, I do," Kayla says as she walks out the door.

Kayla gets into the old Caprice. She wonders about what she told Shelly and if it was the right thing to do. However, she seemed captured by Shelly's calm grace and felt safe in telling her things she usually keeps to herself.

She hopes she didn't screw up as she drives away..

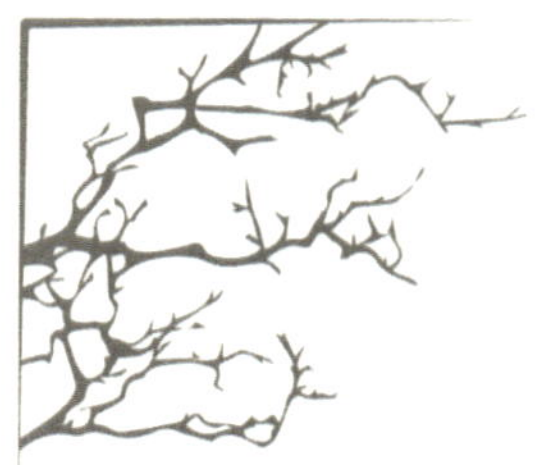

Chapter 22

A growing chill awakens Thomas as snowflakes fall from the sky and settle on his face and clothes.

Where the hell am I, he thinks as he looks at the thin deciduous trees making a "wall" in front of him. The cold grave marker he rests his hand on grabs his attention.

Now he knows where he is.

He gets up and brushes the snow from his hair and clothes. His hand runs along the bottle in his pocket and he reaches in for it, but a pang of guilt hits him. He leaves the bottle where it is.

The morning's drunkenness is wearing off, and he's getting a headache. His thoughts turn to him going over to Shelly's house and remembering how she reacted once she smelled his breath. For the first time in a long time, Thomas feels disappointed in himself. He wonders if he can really move on when all he wants to do is move back. He just doesn't know.

The thoughts churn in his head as he gently kisses his fingers and presses them against the gravestones of the two people he thought he would love and have in his life forever. In his head, he feels like he's communicating with them.

He hears each voice begging him to start living again.

Thomas looks down at the graves and nods his head. He mouths his lips to say, "*I hear you.*"

The phone in his pocket vibrates. He pulls it out and answers it.

"Shea here."

"Thomas, it's Kayla. Ozzie has some news, and he says we need to get right over there," she replies.

What's going on?"

"Not sure. I think our two murders might be connected."

"Okay, I'll be there in about 20."

"Sounds good. Meet you there."

Kayla hangs up. Thomas slowly drops his phone back into his pocket as he stares down at the gravestones.

He feels something has begun to change in him, even though the feeling seems distant. He walks to his pickup and leaves

Kayla sits in the parking lot by the back doors of the Medical Examiner's Office when Thomas pulls up in his pickup. He gets out at the same time Kayla exits her vehicle.

The first thing she notices is how matted down the hair is on the left side of his head.

"Where have you been sleeping?" she asks.

"Huh?" Thomas is confused.

"Your hair. It's all pressed down and looks a little wet," she says.

"I guess I should have looked in the rear-view mirror," he says absentmindedly.

Kayla nods in agreement.

"Let's go in," Thomas says.

"Let's," she agrees after thinking he doesn't look any worse now than he always does.

Ozzie sits behind his neatly kept desk studying reports when Thomas and Kayla enter.

Kayla bounds up to him. Excited to learn new things.

"So what have you got for us today?" she asks.

Ozzie looks up at her and a clearly disheveled Thomas. He would be concerned, but he's also used to Thomas not looking his best nowadays.

"We've got another interesting case, I'm afraid. Have a seat."

Oz motions to the chairs in front of his desk.

They both sit down.

Thomas immediately starts tapping the armrest on his chair ever so softly with his fingers as the urge to get a drink comes over him.

Dr. Ozzie sorts through a couple of files.

He finds what he's looking for and opens it up.

"First off, I went back and checked the body of our beheaded victim with a fine tooth comb."

"Why did you do that?" Kayla asks.

"Well, there's a couple of disturbing similarities between him and the victim found in the wood chipper," Ozzie says.

"Like what?" Thomas asks as he shifts around uncomfortably in his chair.

Ozzie watches as Thomas finally finds a position to sit in. "You okay, Tommy?" he asks him.

"Yea, fine. Just carry on," Thomas replies as he flashes Ozzie *I wish you wouldn't call me that look.*

Ozzie flashes him back with his patented twinkling eyes smile.

"Okay, well, from what I could tell of the wood chipper case, he also died while alert, and there weren't any defensive wounds. That's a little too close for comfort. considering the way our beheaded victim died."

"I can see where you think the guy in the chipper was alive. I mean, his wide eyes tell you that, but how can you tell if our beheaded guy was alive like you mentioned to Josh?" Thomas asks.

Ozzie's face brightens up like he solved a major mystery puzzle. "Blood loss and lack of defensive wounds," he announces.

"Blood loss?" Kayla says in an inquisitive manner.

"Think of a chicken getting its head cut off. Everyone's heard stories about them running around until they squirt all their blood out and die, right?" Ozzie asks.

"Except for Mike the Headless Chicken. That thing lived for about a year and a half," Thomas notes.

"Well, they didn't exactly cut off all of his head. Part of the brain was left in there at the top of the neck, and that's why it kept living," Ozzie counters.

"There are always exceptions to the rule," Thomas says as he smiles back.

"Granted, Tommy. Now may I continue?" Ozzie asks.

Thomas nods his approval.

"So, except for Mike, when you chop off the head of a chicken, its heart is still beating, and that helps drain it of its blood. Which helps preserve the meat during processing and keeps it from getting a metallic or iron taste to it," Ozzie continues.

"I'll keep that in mind next time I butcher a chicken," Thomas says.

"You're sounding a little testy today. You sure you're good?" Ozzie asks.

Thomas sinks in the chair a little bit, his fingers still tapping against the armrest.

"I don't know, Ozzie. Day of reflection, I guess."

"We all get days like that, Thomas," Ozzie replies.

Ozzie using the name Thomas hangs in the air for a moment until Thomas realizes he didn't say, Tommy. He looks at Ozzie and sees the caring in his eyes staring back at him.

"So, to carry on," Ozzie continues, "what's important is that the blood won't drain out like this if the heart were to stop beating. I found less than 1,500 CCs of blood in his system, which is roughly a quart and a half. A man his size typically has around seven quarts of blood in the system. I believe one reason for the increase in blood loss during death was that he was excited and had an accelerated heartbeat and pressure. This would cause more blood to pump out of his system than if he was in a relaxed non-excitable state. At least, that's my conclusion. You can debate it if you wish."

Thomas shakes his head no. "Makes sense to me," he says. "But what are the chances being in the water led to so much blood loss?"

"Good question," Ozzie counters, "Without his heart beating, his arteries and veins would have closed off by the time he was dumped in the water, and only incidental blood loss would have occurred afterward. You wouldn't lose 80 percent of your blood after your heart stops beating unless you were getting squeezed - like if you find yourself under the tires of a bulldozer."

"There's a nice thought," Kayla pipes in.

Thomas' tapping of his fingers picks up a little bit.

"I decided to do some further analysis on the beheading victim's remains, and I came across a small puncture wound that I hadn't noticed before, just below the slicing marks in his neck. When I checked the neck area of our other victim, I found a similar puncture wound."

Dr. Ozzie leans forward to emphasize what he is about to say.

"I believe we have the start of a serial killer on our hands. I've expedited the testing process through toxicology, and we should have something in the next few days," Ozzie says as Thomas keeps on tapping his fingers.

Ozzie looks at Thomas "You sure you're okay?"

Thomas seems surprised.

"Yea, why?" he responds.

Dr. Ozzie looks at his tapping fingers.

It's the first moment Thomas has become aware he's tapping them against the armrest. He stops.

He also needs a drink - bad.

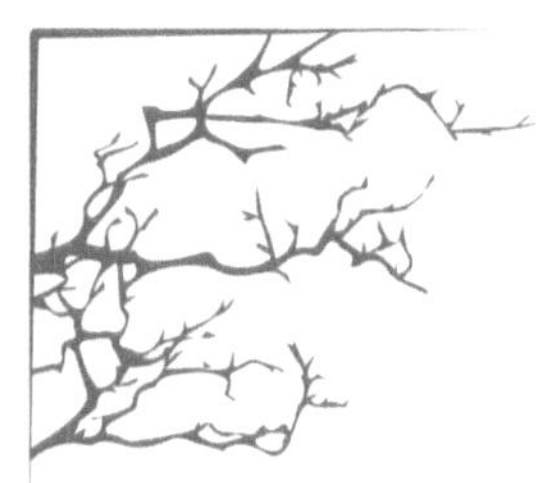

Chapter 23

Kayla pulls in behind Thomas as they head into the police department's back parking lot next to the Cathedral. They meet as they get out of their vehicles and walk quietly together toward the back corner entrance.

Small beads of sweat appear on Thomas' forehead, and he feels like collapsing.

He notices Shelly waiting on the sidewalk wearing a heavy leather motorcycle jacket. She has a bold stance with her chin held high and her shoulders pressed back. She looks like someone who's walked down many roads, mostly dark ones, and she's learned who she is and how to tell quickly how others are.

Something only a cop like Thomas would notice - others would just say she looked tough.

She sees something she likes in the man she sees falling apart. A feeling that's gotten her in trouble before because lost puppies don't always want to be found and cuddled - she's learned that the hard way, too – a few times, but still...

Thomas glances over to Kayla. "Give me a minute."

Kayla nods and keeps on walking. She trades a trusting glance with Shelly as she passes her and heads into police headquarters.

Shelly continues to study Thomas as he walks up to her. She notices how his eyes are more sunken than they were this morning.

She also notices the matted-down hair on one side of his head.

"I want to apologize," she says.

Thomas looks deeply into her eyes. He sees strength in them. A strength he remembers having once. The thought shoots another painful arrow into his heart as he knows the hole is only getting deeper.

He produces a soft regretful smile.

"No need. You were right," he says quietly.

Shelly unconsciously steps up closer to him.

"I lashed out. You came to see how I was doing and I used you as a target for my anger. That's not right." She looks deeply into Thomas' sad eyes. "I've made a commitment to myself to not do that anymore to anyone...and until this morning, I've held true. This whole thing. I never thought something like this would happen to Teddy. He was always so kind."

"Sometimes, these things don't make a lot of sense."

"I guess not. Also, I'm not sure if you know, but as I looked through the paper, I noticed another man was killed yesterday, Troy Englewood."

"That's right," a curious look comes over Thomas' face.

"He worked with Teddy at the prison."

"Did you know him?"

"I met him on a couple of occasions when I helped Teddy with art projects at the prison."

"What did he do?"

"He was a guard. Worked with the most highly dangerous and dysfunctional prisoners to help them integrate into the general population."

Thomas ponders things for a moment.

"Were he and your husband friends?"

"I think they had a mutual respect for each other, but I don't recall them doing anything together outside of work."

"Anything ever happened that would cause someone to do them harm?"

"You think they're connected?"

"That's my first thought."

Shelly seemingly stares into Thomas' chest as she her mind wonders back to a time she has since mostly forgotten.

"A lot of things happen in prison."

Thomas nods, "I know."

She looks up into his face. "Nothing really stands out. They both tried hard to make things better and give direction to prisoners' lives. I can't see anyone wanting to do this to them."

Thomas smiles softly.

"Okay, thanks," he says.

"Sorry."

She really gives Thomas a good looking over and notices he's really looking like a man who needs to sit down.

"You okay?" she asks.

Thomas gives her the most honest look anyone has given her in some time now.

"I don't know," he says.

In an unconscious move, she bends the knuckle on her index finger and pokes it hard enough through Thomas' coat until she feels it press against his belly.

"When was the last time you had a good meal?"

Thomas smiles, and a twinkle appears in his eyes.

"What do you consider a good meal?"

"One that gives your body the nourishment it needs to function properly."

"Beer count?"

"No," she says flatly, "Why don't you come over and I'll fix you something good and nourishing?"

"You know how to fix a good one?" he asks teasingly. An action that surprises him; it's been a long time since he found himself kidding around with a woman - it feels nice.

Shelly shrugs. "If I can't, I know how to order out."

She quickly pulls out her smartphone and shows it to him.

Thomas suddenly hesitates at the thought of going over. *What would going over mean? Would it change my life? Can I change my life?*

He's just not sure he can start over again. He's not sure if he wants to touch another woman the way he wants to touch the woman in front of him ever again - regardless of the permission he felt his wife gave him at the gravesite.

"That sounds nice," he tells her, " but I've got a lot of work to do. How about a rain check?"

Shelly smiles and gives him a slight hug. "Sure. Hey, thanks for coming by to look out for me. I appreciate it."

"I'm sorry I didn't help," Thomas replies.

"No, you did. You really did. Well, anyway, take care."

She starts to walk away, then turns around.

"Hey, if you want, you can stop by anytime; the door's always open, but do me a favor," she says.

"What's that?"

"Don't be drinking. I'd like to get to know the real you. Okay?"

Thomas just nods. He feels a sense of dread that he's making a mistake sweeps over him. Then, she turns around.

"One other thing," she adds.

"What's that?" he replies.

"A shower and clean clothes would be nice, too. You know, before you drop by."

Embarrassment about his unkempt appearance sweeps over him.

He raises his hands, palms up. "You really want *this* to stop by, even in clean clothes?"

She smiles warmly, "Yea, I do."

He watches as she turns back around one last time, wades through the gray slush along the side of the street, and gets into her 4-wheel drive Jeep Patriot.

She flashes a smile and waves as she shifts the Jeep into gear and drives away.

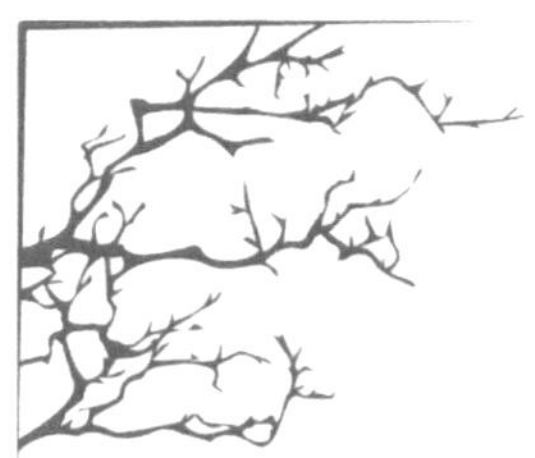

Chapter 24

Kayla sits at her desk going through a file when Thomas enters. He's growing increasingly fidgety as he tries to keep his hands still.

"Got some information back on Englewood's fingerprints, did you know..." she starts to say before Thomas cuts her off.

"That he worked at Black Rock Prison with Teddy Casey."

Kayla looks up, totally surprised.

"How'd you know?"

She notices the twinkle in his eyes; it looks nice. Then it dawns on her.

"She just told you," she deadpans.

"You're good. Ever think of becoming a detective?"

Kayla glances at Thomas' unsteady hands.

"So, what's going on?" she asks.

"What do you mean?"

"Your hands? The finger tapping?"

"Nothing."

"Looks like something."

"It's not."

Kayla firmly sets down the paper in her hand and sternly looks at him.

"Listen, I'm going to tell you something, and I don't care if I get in trouble for it. I gotta say it," she says.

"Okay," he sits down to listen.

"I had choices of assignments when I got promoted to detective, and when I heard you needed a partner, I jumped at the chance."

"Why?" Thomas asks, honestly bewildered.

"Because of the man my dad said you were."

"Your dad? Who's your dad?"

"You don't know him exactly, but he knew you."

Thomas raises an eyebrow, he doesn't quite understand.

"You worked on a case a number of years ago. The Bernard Case."

He instantly recognizes the name.

"Mr. Bernard and my dad were close. My dad always talked about how you solved his murder. You were fair, he'd say, but you also didn't take bullshit from the politicians, religious leaders, or gang-bangers. He said everyone who knew what was going on respected you for that."

The room sits in silence except for the annoying buzz of fluorescent lights hanging from the ceiling.

"Do you mind if I turn off this damn light," she says as she flips her eyes up toward the ceiling.

"No," he says as he turns on the lamp at his desk. "I like lamp light better anyway."

"So do I."

She turns off the overhead lights and then turns on her desk lamp before she sits down and continues.

"This is probably going to hurt, but I'm glad he died before he knew I was going to be your partner. I'm glad because I feel like I'm babysitting you all the time. I'm always covering for you," the frustration builds in her voice. "It's like making sure you get dressed and come to work is part of my job. It's not! I signed on to work with a homicide detective who I thought could teach me how to be the best. Instead, you're showing me how to hold on to a civil service job regardless of how fucked up you are."

She sits, waiting for Thomas to respond, but he just stares back at her.

"You have to make a decision," she says. "You need to figure out whether you are going to completely give up or if you are going to fight like the man my dad said you were. You need to make a decision soon, very soon, because if you don't, I'm going to ask to be reassigned before something happens that could affect my career."

"I wouldn't do anything to hurt you."

"What you are doing already hurts me. You need to get control of your demons. Do you hear me?" she begs.

Thomas slowly nods his head in agreement, "I hear you."

"So, anything else?" he asks.

"I called over to Black Rock. The superintendent agreed to see us first thing in the morning."

"Good."

"It'll be an earlier start than usual, he gets in at 6:00 am."

"That's fine."

"You'll be up?" she asks.

"Yea."

"Promise?"

"Kayla, I heard what you said. I'll be up."

"I hope so."

Thomas flashes her a *"you really don't know me yet look."*

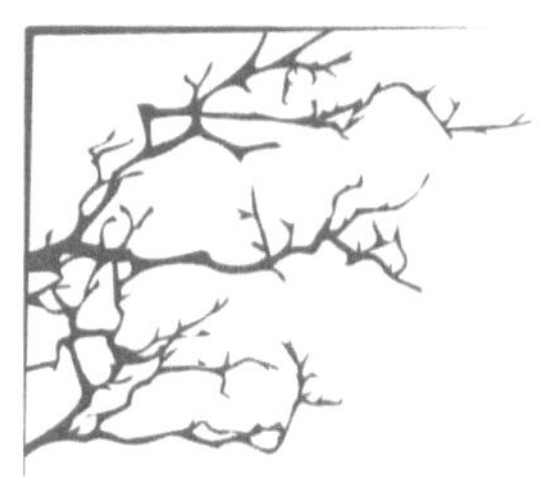

Chapter 25

Shelly decided the best way to take her mind off of what was happening after her sidewalk visit with Thomas was to stop at the Arts-R-Us store on Main Street. It sits among the turn-of-20th Century buildings lining the streets of the Allentown District near where Thomas usually goes to drown himself in alcohol.

The store gives her a special kind of relief as she browses new sculpturing equipment on display. She especially likes how it's one of the best art supply stores in the country, and it's only a mile away from her home. Just far enough to get a good walk on days when she isn't driving. Which are most days.

She is so absorbed in all the wonderful things around her that she doesn't even notice the pea-green Subaru Outback parked across the street or the man sitting in it watching her every move.

Brian was surprised when he saw Shelly standing outside police headquarters next to the cathedral. He figured he'd run out through the vestry and get into the parish car to follow where she was going.

What he didn't notice was Father Isaiah working at his desk. He hears Brian rush through the vestry and out the kitchen door. He goes to the window to watch him jump into the Subaru and speed out of the parking lot.

Brian was in a hurry because he'd been having a hard time finding out exactly where Shelly lived. New York State doesn't allow certain information like phone numbers and personal addresses to be published about correctional officers. It's a way to keep them safe from cons seeking revenge once released from prison, and he knew he had to follow her to find out what he needed to know.

He just couldn't believe his good luck.

Through the window, Brian watches as Shelly happily carries some new blades and chisels to the checkout counter. She gets into an animated conversation with the store clerk. He figures they're probably talking about what new items will be coming in or what training programs the store's resident artists will be offering over the winter. Things he figured artists like her would talk about with someone working at an art supply store.

Shelly flashes a big warm smile over something that was said. He remembers that smile. At first, he loved it. The sight of her smile seemingly made the room a more warm and loving place, but that changed over time. When he would tell her about one of the prisoners and how dangerous he thought she was, Shelly would flash that *warm* smile and tell him he was sure he was wrong.

Her smile. Her condescending "you don't know enough, and I know more" goddamn smile now made him clench his teeth and fists. He couldn't wait until the smile was gone.

He watches Shelly put the supplies she bought into her colorful hemp bag and walks out. She dodges slush piles and dances around road-salt puddles to get back to her Jeep.

Brian follows behind her as she takes off, careful not to get too close.

They snake through West Side streets until Shelly pulls into the driveway of her home. Brian pulls into a parking space on the street a couple of houses down.

Shelly grabs the bag out of the Jeep, walks up the porch steps, and enters her house.

A smile grows on Brian's face as he starts to think about what he should do to her. He hasn't figured it out yet, but he's sure it'll be good.

That is, it'd be good if he finds a way to make peace with his soul when all this is over. A peace he hopes will allow him to escape an everlasting hell like it did once before in his life.

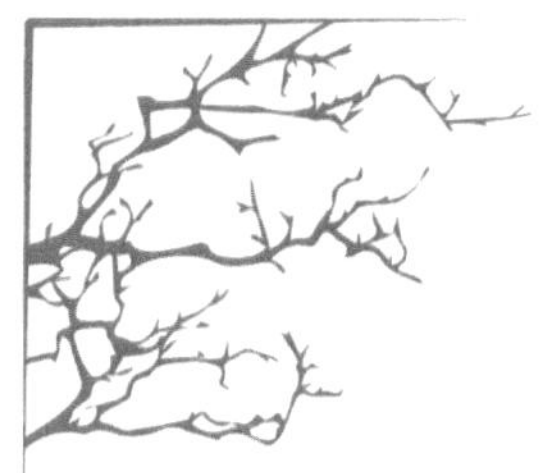

Chapter 26

Thomas finds himself back on the breakwall separating the Black Rock Canal from the Niagara River. He walks out until he finds a tiny sandy beach where the wall zig-zags about a mile from shore. As he steps down onto the sand, he can feel his shoes sink into the softness. He looks at white clouds billowing above the darkness over the lake. A slightly warm breeze caresses his face.

He has always loved moments like this. Standing alone in the darkness against the elements out on the water. He remembers as a young man how this feeling used to give him strength and hope when life was beginning. It was his place of solace on the river.

He raises his face to the wind and darkness in hopes those feelings will once again come back to propel him forward. He's not sure it will, but he hopes so.

Instead, the urge to head to Shane's for a nightcap creeps into his head. He knows if he goes he'll be there for a while. Quite possibly too long to get up early to go meet the superintendent.

The desire inflames his brain and makes his gut hurt. This is not the type of feeling he was hoping for out here.

Maybe it is too late, he thinks. *Maybe I won't come back from this.*

Suddenly, another urge takes over. A need to be with his mom. Thomas flips the collar of his coat up as he steps back up on the breakwall and heads back to his truck in Broderick Park.

Nurse Marcie is working her usual spot at the nurse's station when she's not making rounds. Her face brightens as Thomas gets off an elevator and walks over.

"We might have some good news for you, Detective," she beams.

"What's that?" he replies.

"We've been noticing an uptick in brain activity in your mother. There might be a chance she'll become lucid sometime over the next few days."

"I didn't think that was possible."

"It is, but…"

"But what?"

"There's also a serious downside to her waking up," she says carefully.

"What would that be?"

"It usually means she's at the end. She might come alert for a little while and then she'll probably slip away rapidly."

Thomas takes a moment to digest this information.

"Is there a way of knowing when she'll regain consciousness?"

"Not really. Again, we're just hoping she does because signs point that way. We're not absolutely sure she will or when, but I wanted you to be aware of the possible change in her condition."

"I need to be here if it happens," he says, his voice shaking a little."

"I'll make sure you'll get notified right away if she starts to come out of it."

"I'd really appreciate that, Nurse Marcie."

"You know, at this point, Marcie is fine," she says with a smile.

He sticks out his hand, and Marcie grabs and shakes it.

"Call me Thomas," he says with a smile back.

"Okay, Thomas."

"I'm going to go sit with her for a while, okay?"

"Sure, you know the drill."

"That I do."

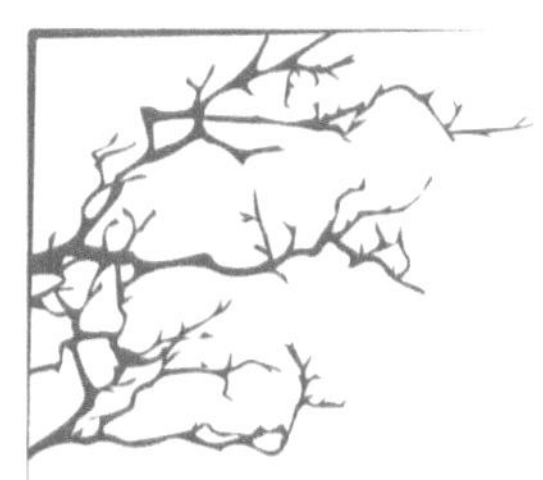

Chapter 27

The imposing red Medina-stoned structure secured with razor-wire fencing reminds Thomas of watching old black and white Boris Karloff's Frankenstein movies with his mom as a child on New Year's Eve. They would wrap themselves up in a blanket with a big bowl of popcorn as they waited to get scared to death while watching what was happening in and around the castle.

Thomas is pretty sure any prisoner coming here probably feels the same way they did as he and Kayla walked up the path to the iron-gated heavy oak doors.

They pull out their badges, rap on the door, and get let in.

"Detectives Shea and Harrison, Buffalo Homicide, we're here to see Superintendent Trowbridge," Thomas states matter-of-factually. Actually, Kayla's impressed. He looks good, well-rested, clean, and a little more assertive. *I like it,* she thinks approvingly.

The guard nods toward a thick plastic window with another guard sitting behind it.

"Sign in over there," he says.

They step up to the front counter.

"I need your weapons. Keep 'em holstered," the guard at the window says like she has said it eleven thousand times since she started working here, and only got a few more months until she retires kind-of-way.

Thomas and Kayla slide their holstered weapons through an opening at the bottom of the window.

The guard fills out a short form and motions to the lockers behind her. "They'll be stored in one of those. Locker number is on the form," she says. She pushes the forms through the small window. "Don't forget 'em when you leave."

A third guard by the door leading inside the prison motions them over.

"I'll take you to the Superintendent's office," he says.

They follow the third guard into a sterile hallway leading to equally sterile administration offices. The guard leads them through the door with the name Superintendent stenciled into the frosty glass.

The guard greets the receptionist.

"Detectives from Buffalo Homicide," he says with as much excitement as the guard at the window.

The receptionist smiles warmly at Thomas and Kayla. "He's expecting you," she says before looking at the guard. "Can you take them out to Greenhouse number four? The superintendent is out there."

"Sure," the guard replies. The receptionist and the guard exchange glances like he might be back after he drops these two off, or so the thought comes to Thomas' mind. But who knows, he could be wrong.

The guard leads Thomas and Kayla across a windy open yard to a magnificent 40' x 120' commercial greenhouse. Warmth and humidity envelopes them as they enter and walk down an aisle of Romaine lettuce growing hydroponically until they reach Superintendent Trowbridge. He's standing with a couple of inmates inspecting freshly cut lettuce on a table next to a large fish tank. He looks up to see the guard leading the two detectives to him.

"You must be the detectives from Buffalo Homicide," Trowbridge says as Thomas and Kayla draw near. "Shea and Harrison?"

"Correct. I'm Shea, this is Harrison," Thomas states as he looks at the lettuce in Trowbridge's hands. "Kind of early for office hours, isn't it?"

"Busy day today. We've got a group from the American Hydroponic Society coming in a couple of hours to inspect our operation. We are up for Gold Certification status, and things have to be ready."

"This is a pretty extensive operation you've got here. Is this all for feeding the prisoners?" Kayla asks.

"Oh, no. We also ship fresh produce to soup kitchens, food pantries, and group homes in the area. Actually, that's how all this got started. A group of superintendents and members from the community banded together to raise food on prison grounds to help feed the hungry. I started one at Willard Correctional Facility in Central New York before I was reassigned to take over here," Trowbridge explains.

"And it's the inmates that do the work?" Kayla asks.

"They pretty much run the entire show here. It provides an opportunity for them to learn new skills while doing something positive for the community. Much of the food goes directly to the neighborhoods where many of our inmates come from; so they get the sense they are making the lives of family members and friends better, too. It's really a win-win," Trowbridge says proudly.

The large tank with fish swimming in it captures Kayla's eye. "What's this for?" she asks.

"This is part of the ecosystem we've established to fertilize and grow produce while also growing Tilapia to harvest. It provides an additional source of protein for our hungry and struggling neighbors. The fish survive off of the waste produced by the plants and the plants survive off the waste the fish produce. It's a very symbiotic relationship and it works well year-round."

"Very interesting," Kayla says. She's impressed.

Trowbridge looks back at Thomas. "Your partner said it was urgent, and this is the only time slot I've got open today. So, what can I do for you?"

"Can we talk in private?" Thomas asks.

"Certainly," Trowbridge responds. He looks at the two inmates who have been helping him this morning. "Could you please excuse us for a few minutes?"

The inmates walk to another part of the greenhouse to inspect other plants.

"We actually came to talk about two former employees: Teddy Casey and Troy Englewood," Thomas says.

"I never knew them personally, but I've been hearing their names being bandied about in the hallways," Trowbridge says. "What can I help with?"

"Well, I guess we'll start with what you've been hearing," Thomas says.

"Not much, really. People are shocked," Trowbridge replies.

"The only connection we know of between them is here. Is there anything you can think of that might help explain what is going on?" Thomas asks.

"If the connection truly is this prison, then, quite honestly, your guess would be as good as mine. There are a lot of good people housed here who've just done misguided things and are harmless, but then there are some who have sick minds who also enjoy doing evil things. Could it be an ex-con? It could," Trowbridge replies.

Kayla pipes in. "Anybody you know that you've had here who enjoys mutilating people?"

"Unfortunately, I've met quite a few over the years, but none here. At least not yet. I just got here a couple of months ago to take over the operation after the former superintendent retired and moved to rural Alaska," Trowbridge replies as he picks up another head of lettuce to inspect.

"Alaska!" Thomas blurts out.

"He's Intuit. Wanted to go back home," Trowbridge replies.

Thomas nods. *Makes sense,* he thinks.

"Is it possible to talk to him?" Thomas asks.

"Possible, but not likely. His plan was to go into the wilderness for a full year to restore his spirit. You'll need a dog sled and a good pair of snow shoes to reach him."

"Yea, you're right, not likely," Thomas adds.

Kayla looks at Trowbridge. "Has anybody mentioned anyone who would have had some connection to Casey and Englewood?"

Trowbridge inspects the root structure of a head of Romaine lettuce as he thinks. "I heard Casey worked with many of the women here to help build up their self-esteem and open their minds to other ways of thinking. He was considered one of the good guys. Troy, on the other hand, was a guard. His training and outlook were...a little bit different than Ted's. The residents often didn't think was one of the good guys, but that's to be expected. Keeping order around here can be challenging at times"

"Do you know of any incidents or mishaps they would have been involved in together?" Thomas asks as he watches Trowbridge expertly twist the head of lettuce around.

Trowbridge shakes his head. "As I've mentioned, I've only been here a short time, and I'm still getting to know

the lay of the land, so to speak."

"Well, if you think of anything, you'll get in touch?" Thomas asks.

"Most definitely," Trowbridge responds. "Hey, grab some lettuce on the way out. It's delicious."

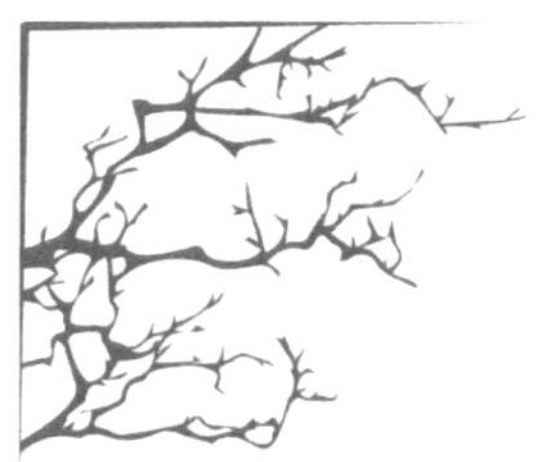

Chapter 28

The soft glow from the cathedral lights filters into the darkness between the cathedral and police headquarters. Feeling lost, Thomas sits back in his wooden desk chair, staring out the window at the grand edifice.

Kayla walks in, carrying some papers.

"I've got the address of Jeff Englewood's friend Debbie Hale. You want to go tonight or tomorrow?" she asks.

Thomas remains undisturbed - his mind is someplace far, far, away.

Kayla clears her throat and speaks louder, "Thomas!".

He snaps around like he was startled awake while sleeping.

"What?"

"You okay?" she asks.

"Can people stop asking me that question?"

"Well...are you?"

"I don't know, Kayla," he says as he rises. "I've got to go out."

"Shane's?"

"What? No...I don't know, but I gotta go."

"So we'll do Debbie Hale tomorrow?"

"Who?" Thomas responds.

"Never mind. I'll see you tomorrow."

"Yea, okay. Thanks."

Kayla watches Thomas storm out like he's on a mission; worry covers her face.

Old man winter is bearing down again by the time Thomas gets downstairs and walks out of Police Headquarters into a snow squall with howling winds. Thomas walks over to the back parking lot. He stops to look up at the Cathedral's single tall spire standing strong against the storm.

He walks around to the front of the cathedral and slowly climbs the steps to the heavy large wooden doors with brass handles. He pulls on a handle and enters; hopeful this visit will make him feel like the last one did.

Brian watches the door close behind Thomas as he stands in the shadow of a large pine tree on the cathedral's front lawn. The sight of Thomas entering the Cathedral disturbs him. Has Thomas discovered something about Brian's involvement in the case or is he jut coming in for another visit? The need to know draws him up the stone stairs to the wooden doors with brass handles.

Thomas moves slowly down the right side aisle until he gets to the Statue of Mary gazing benevolently downward at him. Burning candles cast a soft glow over her feet.

He takes a deep breath and stares at the statue's soothing face. Then, he walks over to a pew and sits. He settles into the pew and folds his hands on his lap like he's getting ready to wait for something to happen.

He hears the echo of one of the large wooden front doors opening and closing in the empty cathedral.

Thomas turns slightly to watch Brian enter the main cathedral wearing his long black coat and hat. He quickly removes his hat, dips his finger into a bowl of Holy Water attached to the entrance's frame, and does the sign of the cross over his chest with his wet finger.

Then he swiftly moves along the right side aisle past Thomas. He acts like he doesn't notice Thomas as he moves past him and stops at the feet of the Statue of Mary. Taking a bill out of his pocket, Brian folds it and slides it through a slot in the money collector sitting in the front middle of the table with candles.

Pulling out one of the long match sticks, Brian strikes it against a rough edge on the side of the money box to make a flame. He uses the flame to light a candle. Then he drops to his knees and acts like he's silently praying when he's actually taking Thomas all in.

He feels something strange coming from Thomas. Like he's just another lost and hurting soul who wanders in here every now and then in search of comfort and safety just like he had a couple of years before.

Thomas sits quietly, looking up at the main altar while keeping the sight of Brian in the corner of his eye. He notices how methodical Brian seemed to be as he went through the motions of lighting the candle and getting on his knees to pray. Like he knows what he's doing and what should be done – all the things he didn't pay attention to when he was a boy.

He wonders if the man he's watching pray has the answers he's seeking or if he's just as screwed up as he is. Either way, the kneeling man seems to be in a better place than the one Thomas is in right now.

After a moment, Brian rises and does the cross over his chest again. He turns to walk back down the aisle.

Thomas calls out to him. "Excuse me," he says softly.

Brian's heart jumps in his chest. Maybe this hurting man sitting in the pew is the sign he's been looking for!

He slowly turns towards Thomas.

"Yes?" Brian responds.

"Can I talk to you for a second?"

Brian can hardly hold back the joy he is feeling.

"Me?" He says as he looks at Thomas.

"Yes, you," Thomas replies.

Brian feels a lump growing in his throat. "What can I do for you?"

"You seem like you know about all this stuff - the statues, prayers, things like that," Thomas says.

"I know some things," Brian replies.

"Can you teach me about them?"

The happiness flows out of Brian's body. He was right, this wandering and damaged soul is looking for comfort and safety just like he had hoped. Brian slides in next to Thomas on the pew.

"What is it you want to know?" he asks.

Sadness fills Thomas' face as he glances around.

"I should know these things. When I was a boy, my Uncle Joe would bring me here. We'd sit over there on the other side." Thomas looks around like he might see his uncle appear in the pew where they sat before continuing. "I didn't come for Jesus or God, I came because I wanted to spend time with my uncle."

He pauses like he's struggling for answers. "I'm not sure why I'm here now," he adds.

His words touch Brian in ways he didn't expect. He remembers when he first came to these doors a few years ago searching for a way out of the darkness that enveloped his life as a boy. He was wandering then looking to escape the hell he lived on a daily basis. He remembers how Father Isaiah came to his side and softly spoke to him. The kindness Father Isaiah showed was unlike any he had ever experienced with an adult person. He was used to being banished by people in the neighborhood, mostly adults and parents, and wasn't used to an adult being kind to him with no strings attached.

Brian thinks of the words and actions Father Isaiah used to get him to open up. An opening up that led to a massive change in his life, at least for a little while.

"Start with your feelings," Brian says gently.

"Feel...that I haven't done for some time. It doesn't pay in my line of work."

"Which is?" Brian asks like he doesn't know who Thomas really is.

"Homicide Detective, Buffalo. I work next door."

"We all feel, Detective, even when we think we don't. What are you feeling right now?"

Thomas drops his head, his despair oozes out.

"I feel like my world is falling apart and I'm not sure if I care."

Again, his words touch Brian's heart. He never thought he'd be in a position to feel cops were human. To him, as a boy growing up, they were part of the enemy. Someone you feared not because they represented the law, but because they used the law to represent their own various interests out on the streets. It was hard to find a good one in Brian's world, but he knew of one or two.

Now, he's starting to feel like he's found another one. He senses something good in Thomas. Something he likes.

"Why wouldn't you care?" he asks.

Thomas leans back against the hard pew and looks up at the gracefully arched ceiling.

"Life's finally drained it all out of me," Thomas replies. "I'm empty inside."

Brian can see the tears welling up in the bottom of Thomas' eyes. Thomas quickly looks away and uses the sleeve of his coat to wipe them from his face. The pain Brian sees in Thomas reminds him of the pain he's he has because of Jennifer's death. It makes him suddenly feel connected to the man he also knows he should stay away from as much as possible in order to avenge her death.

But this sign from God compels him forward.

"Why?" Brian asks.

Thomas shrugs his shoulders a little. "One day I had everything to live for and then one day I didn't."

Brian gently looks at Thomas. "What happened?"

"Life," Thomas says.

"Life?"

"The one thing I've learned about life is that at the end of the day, we're all vulnerable and incapable of stopping bad things from happening to us. It doesn't matter what good we think we've done or what good we've actually done. No one earns a guarantee that life won't bring bad times. No one."

Brian doesn't believe this for a second. His mind screams that of course doing good helps. It takes some of the burden and pain away. You have to do good after you've done bad to get over doing bad! But, he knows he shouldn't challenge Thomas. That's how Father Isaiah treated Brian. He never challenged Brian's thoughts and said he had to think another way. Instead, he let him talk and say the things he needed to say. Brian decides to do the same with Thomas.

Thomas gets a little uncomfortable being as open as he's doing; especially with someone he doesn't know at all.

"Well, anyway, I guess I've said enough," Thomas says.

"You didn't ask your questions."

"Yea, I didn't. I don't know, I'm just searching, I guess," Thomas laments.

"How have you been searching?" Brian asks.

Thomas taps the bottle in his coat pocket. "Drinking, mainly."

"I've gone down that road. Spent years lost doing drugs and drinking. I know what you're going through."

"So what do I do?"

"Quit running and start searching for your answer."

Thomas produces a melancholic smile.

"I thought that's what I was doing."

"Being lost doesn't necessarily mean you're searching," Brian says.

Thomas softly smiles. "I guess you're right there. By the way, my name's Thomas Shea. Sorry for unloading on you."

Brian takes Thomas' outstretched hand and grasps it.

"Brian Mulroney," he says.

They shake hands.

"I saw you replacing the candles the other night. What is it you do here?" Thomas asks.

"I mostly help fill the gaps in the workload created by the absence of priests nowadays."

"I guess we all need people who can do that," Thomas says. He pulls out a business card and hands it to Brian.

"You know, I'm glad I met you. You've made me feel a little better," Thomas adds.

"Thank you," Brian responds. "Do you have another card?"

Thomas pulls out another card and hands it to him. Brian takes a pen and writes his name and number on the back of it.

"If you ever need a kindred spirit to talk to, call me," Brian tells Thomas as he hands the card back to him.

"Thanks, Brian," Thomas replies as he gets up. "I need to go check on someone. Good meeting you."

Brian watches as Thomas heads out. Then, he leans back to ponder how the Good Lord works.

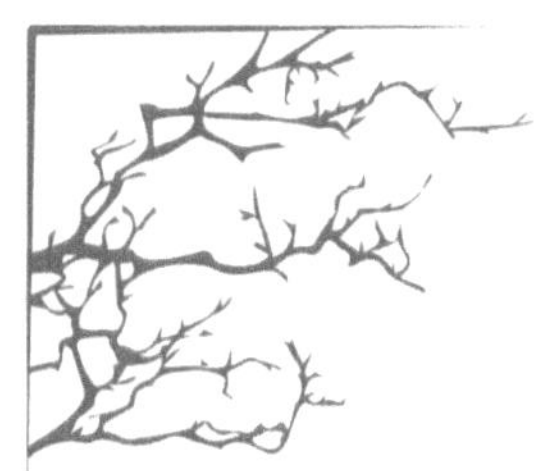

Chapter 29

Nurse Marcie pushes a medicine cart from room to room as Thomas exits the elevator.

"Hi, Marcie," Thomas says quietly.

"Oh, hi, Thomas. I didn't think you were coming tonight," Marcie replies.

"Seems like the best place to be. Been thinking about what you told me all day. How's she doing? Getting any more awake?" Thomas asks.

"No, I'm sorry. There is some extra brain activity, but it hasn't picked up enough to cause her to wake up," Marcie replies.

"Okay, I'm just going to sit with her for a while, okay?"

"Of course, Thomas." She notices he's sober, she likes it.

Thomas slips into his mother's room. All he hears are the beeping of monitors and the whooshing sound of the respirator's diaphragm pulling air in and pushing it out again.

Thomas sits down in the faux-leather chair and settles in for another long night by the shell of his mother. Visions of his daughter, wife, Shelly, Kayla, and Brian percolate in his mind. Each takes a turn appearing and fading from his view. Each call to him to do something to save himself and each call pushes that thought deeper into his consciousness as he drifts away into sleep.

As the morning sun shines through the window, Nurse Marcie enters Thomas' mother's room dressed in street clothes. She sets a cup of coffee and a muffin on the table next to a sleeping Thomas. Then she gently shakes him until his eyes open.

"Hey, time to get up. I'm getting ready to go, but I brought you some coffee and a muffin," she says.

Thomas looks at the coffee and muffin on the clean plastic table top. A tabletop that's usually filled with leftover wrappers and maybe a small bottle of booze when he comes in after a bender. He kind of likes how it looks. He also kind of likes how good he's feeling without a hangover - for the second day in a row.

"Hey, thanks," the appreciation sparkles in his eyes.

Suddenly, a seven-year-old girl with curly red hair and a freckled face pops into the doorway.

"Hey, Mom. You ready?" the girl asks.

Thomas looks at Marcie. "Yours?"

"My daughter, Tracy," she says proudly. "Tracy, this is Detective Shea."

The little girl suddenly turns shy. "Hello," Tracy almost whispers.

A warm smile crosses Thomas' face. "Hello," he says back.

Tracy grabs Marcie's hand and tugs on it a little.

"We're going Christmas shopping today," Marcie says.

"Oh, that's always fun," Thomas replies.

"I can't wait until it's over."

"C'mon, mommy," Tracy tugs at her hand some more.

"All right, sweetie," she says. She looks at Thomas, "you going to be okay?"

Thomas chuckles. *How many times am I going to hear this question?* he asks himself.

"I'll be fine. You two have fun," he replies.

"Okay," Marcie smiles at him. "I'll check in on your mom when I get in tonight."

"I know you will. Thanks."

Tracy tugs on her hand again, and this time, she allows Tracy to lead her out of the room as she waves goodbye to Thomas.

The morning sun had risen further up in the sky by the time Thomas got back to his apartment from the long-term care facility to take a shower and change his clothes. The mess and emptiness grab him as he steps inside. He feels disgusted as he looks at the living conditions he's come to find acceptable.

He starts to clean.

First things first, he starts grabbing the clothes flung all around the place and piles them on the couch. He disappears into the bedroom, returning moments later with a laundry hamper - in goes the clothes.

Next, the dishes, glasses, and rotting food strewn on every tabletop all need to go. He runs back and forth between the kitchen and living room as he picks all of it up and takes it into the kitchen for cleaning or disposal.

Soon, the kitchen table is piled high with dirty plates, glasses, pans, and pots. Thomas turns on the faucet, pours soap into the dishpan, and fills it up with steamy hot water.

Then, a moment of truth arrives; he opens the cupboard and looks at the bottle of old granddad. Slowly he grabs the bottle and unscrews the top. He puts it to his nose and inhales. He closes his eyes; the temptation is strong.

The doorbell rings.

Thomas recaps the bottle and puts it back in the cupboard. He walks out of the kitchen and strides across the now much cleaner living room, and answers the door.

There stands Kayla, fumbling with her keys.

"You're awake!" She's genuinely surprised.

"True," he replies.

Thomas stands aside so Kayla can enter. She looks around in total amazement.

"Wow, it's clean!" she's astonished.

"You sure you don't want to take that lieutenant's test?" Thomas deadpans.

"Don't be a pain in my ass. What's up?"

"Just time for a change."

"Change. Good word. You haven't moved on to something stronger than alcohol?" she asks.

"Now, don't you be a pain in my ass!"

They both share a laugh.

"Really, I'm impressed," Kayla says sincerely.

"As you know, that's important to me," Thomas says back.

Kayla rolls her eyes.

"All right, how about getting down to business?" she says as she looks at Thomas.

"Sure. What are we doing?"

"Debbie Hale," Kayla responds.

"What about her?"

"We're going to interview her this morning. I called her, and she said to meet her at the lodge at Chestnut Ridge."

"Right. We should do that," Thomas says as he grabs his coat.

Before long, Thomas and Kayla sit with Debbie and Jeff at one of the large wooden tables near the huge fireplace in the Chestnut Ridge Park lodge.

"You didn't see or hear anything?" Thomas asks Debbie.

"Nothing," Debbie replies. "He helped me like he usually did; he helped everybody."

"We've been extremely proud of him lately," Jeff adds sadly.

The statement catches Kayla's attention. "Lately?" she says to Jeff.

"Well...up until a couple of years ago, he was kind of a jerk. He drank a lot and didn't really treat people well, especially his family," Jeff explains.

Thomas picks up on Kayla's curiosity. "What made him change?" he asks Jeff.

Jeff thinks for a moment, then just shrugs his shoulders. "I don't know. One day he was totally different. It was like he saw the light, and it made him change. He started to appreciate the things he seemed to ignore and abuse before."

"When would you say this change took place, exactly?" Thomas asks.

Jeff struggles to remember. "He started to change in early summer a couple of years ago. All of a sudden, it was like he was happy I was around." He starts to cry as Debbie reaches around and holds him. "It was like I finally had a dad," he adds.

"Did something happen at the prison?" Thomas asks Jeff.

"I don't know. Dad never talked much about what happened over there, and when he came home bothered by something, it was often best if we didn't ask about it or hang around him."

Thomas and Kayla rise.

"Well, thanks. I'm sorry for your loss," He says to a clearly distraught son and the girl who's comforting him.

As they head out of the park in Thomas' pickup, he turns to Kayla.

"A good man becomes a bad man, and a bad man becomes a good man. What would cause something like that?" he asks her.

"Something life-changing. What did Mrs. Cortland say the timeline was for the transformation of her husband?"

"I'm not sure if we actually narrowed that down to a specific time."

"We probably should. Now a good time?" he asks.

"Sure," she replies.

Thomas raps on the front door of Shelly's house as Kayla peers through a narrow window next to the door.

"I don't think she's here," she says.

"Maybe she's around back."

"Let's check it out."

Thomas and Kayla head down the steps as the woman next door steps out of her house.

"You looking for Shelly again?" she asks from her porch.

"Yea," Thomas replies.

"She's at Delaware Park. The Rose Garden area. They're doing the ice sculpture contest today."

"Okay, Thanks," Thomas says.

Kayla whispers over to Thomas as they walk away. "She sure does keep an eye on things."

"That she does," Thomas responds.

After a drive down tree-lined streets devoid of leaves, they arrive at the Rose Garden area of Delaware Park as the sun sets over the horizon. There are numerous artists showing off their ice sculptures to the many aficionados mulling around in appreciation of their talents. Globe antique-style street lamps from the late 1800s shine off the ice crystal sculptures glistening on tabletops in the growing night.

Shelly is surrounded by several people who are awed by her rendition of an eagle in flight. She sees Thomas and Kayla walking towards her and breaks off the conversation.

A wide smile grows on her face as she notices how good Thomas looks.

"I didn't think you'd be showing up," Shelly says as they arrive at her side.

"We're not really here for the show," Thomas responds.

"You're not? That's disappointing. Why are you here?"

"To ask a quick question," Thomas says. "When exactly would you say that change occurred in your ex-husband?"

"A couple of years ago."

"But when?"

Shelly thinks hard for a moment.

" I would have to say in June two summers ago."

"By any chance, did he go camping or do any traveling? Especially with Troy Englewood?" Kayla asks.

"No, not that I remember, and since I love camping, I would have remembered him going without me. Why?"

"We're just trying to find out why your husband and Englewood were murdered. There's gotta be a connection besides just working at the same place for a while," Thomas says.

"Like I said before, a lot of things go on in a prison. Teddy would only talk about things I personally saw and wanted to discuss afterward, but I didn't see anything that would cause an ex-con to go after him," Shelly says. "But, you know, that still doesn't mean something didn't happen, just nothing I know about."

"Well, if you do, call. Okay?" Thomas says to her.

"Yea."

Thomas and Kayla start to leave.

"Thomas," Shelly calls out.

Thomas turns around. She motions for him to come closer, which he gladly does.

She looks hopefully at Thomas. "I was just wondering, are you doing anything Saturday?" she asks.

"Besides working homicide and taking care of some personal business, no."

"Do you go cross-country skiing?"

"Used to, but it's been a long time."

"Would you like to ski the meadow with me? It's an easy trail, and I'd like the company," she says with a soft smile.

Thomas smiles back. "Actually, I would like that."

"How about Saturday morning at 8:30? We'll meet on Ring Road by the Zoo entrance."

"Sounds good."

Shelly reaches up around his neck and gives him a hug.

"Remember, no booze," she whispers into his ear.

"Understood," he replies.

Thomas and Kayla walk away back toward the pickup as Shelly starts conversing with other aficionados of ice art.

Kayla leans in close to Thomas as they walk.

"Does she know what she's getting ready to adopt?" she says in a low voice.

"I doubt it. I don't even know anymore myself."

Light snow starts to fall on Christmas ornaments popping up on lawns throughout the neighborhood Thomas is driving through.

Kayla sits next to him.

"So, now what?" she says.

"What else connects the two?"

"I've gone through the files. Englewood was an outdoor type who liked hunting, fishing and working on vehicles and equipment. Casey was more cerebral, he was into creating lasting impressions through art."

"They were both into nature."

"Weak."

"Grabbing."

"I can tell."

Thomas flicks on the radio. Andy Williams singing "It's The Most Wonderful Time of the Year" comes on.

"There's got to be someone or something that connects them," he says.

"Or both."

"Or both," Thomas says in agreement.

They emerge from the neighborhood of stately houses with large holiday displays, and in a short time, they end up stopped at the light at the corner of Franklin and Tupper Streets.

On the corner sits Shane's.

Thomas looks over to see a single acoustical guitar player on the stage in the window. It's moments like these that Thomas likes to sit in a dark corner to listen until his mind weakens from alcohol and shuts down enough for him to nod out. A yearning creeps into his eyes. His knuckles turn white as he grips the steering wheel hard while he fights the urge. Kayla notices before she looks up at the stop light.

"Green," she states.

Thomas turns to look at her.

"What?"

She nods forward.

"The light. It turned green."

Thomas forces himself to look straight ahead and drive instead of pulling over.

"You wanna come over for pizza and a movie?" she asks.

Thomas ponders this for a moment.

"Nah, I've got more cleaning to do."

"You sure?"

Thomas stares into her eyes as feels his inner strength coming back. It makes him think he might have a chance to regain control of his life after all.

"Yea, actually, I am."

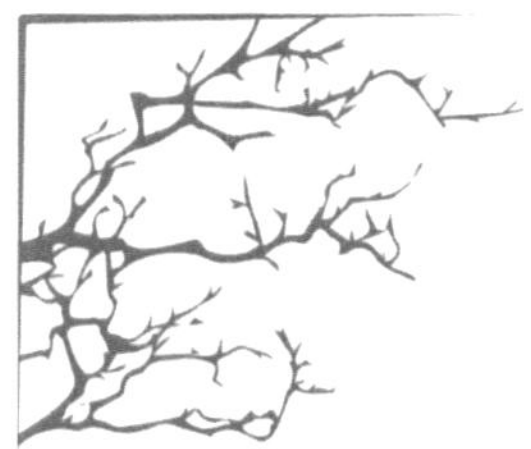

Chapter 30

Instead of heading home to clean more, Thomas decides he wants to talk about things. Even that short talk with Brian the other night helped him to feel a little better, and a little better at a time is better than nothing at all.

That's why he called Brian and asked to meet at the outdoor ice rinks of the RiverWorks complex situated along the Buffalo River just south of the cereal plant and across the river from Conway Park, where Thomas played ball for his dad as a boy. A soft breeze blows off the lake past the old grain elevator that's been repurposed into a towering replica of a six-pack of Labatt's Blue Beer cans and onto ice rinks filled with skaters competing in a yearly hockey-like charitable event called "Scoring for Hope".

Thomas and Brian sit in the stands watching players trying to score on tiny nets about six inches high and four feet across. Thomas holds a cardboard cup full of steaming hot coffee in his hands. He takes a sip.

"Every day is pretty much the same. I get up, snatch a drink, go to work, and grab drinks during the day whenever I can. I can hardly wait until I leave work so I can spend the rest of my night drinking myself into a state of semi-consciousness. It's all I've done since...."

Thomas grows quiet.

Brian speaks softly. "Since what?"

Thomas takes another sip and stares off into the distance at Conway Field on the other side of the frozen river.

"Forget it. I'm unloading again."

Brian places his hand on Thomas' shoulder.

"Isn't that why you called me?" he asks. "I know it's why I came."

"It's not something I do. We've all got our struggles," Thomas continues.

"It's important not to struggle alone."

"It's also important not to be a burden."

Brian nods knowingly. "Even to yourself," he says.

They sit in silence as the sounds of kids laughing and screaming fill the air.

Finally, Thomas turns to Brian.

"What's your story?' he asks.

Brian shrugs.

"I guess not much different than yours in a lot of ways," Brian begins, "I spent a lot of time struggling to move ahead from something and leave the past behind."

"What were you trying to leave behind?" Thomas asks.

"Me."

"You?"

"Yea."

"I'm not sure I understand," Thomas says.

"It's kind of a long story."

"I've got a little time," Thomas responds. "I'd like to know who the guy is who's trying to help me."

"You really want to know?"

"I would."

A great sadness descends on Brian's face as he stares into nothing.

"I was born into a cold home," he says.

Thomas is not sure what that means.

"You had no heat?" he responds.

Brian smiles softly. "Sometimes, but that's not what I mean. You can have a cold house and still have a warm home, but you can't have a warm one without someone there to keep it that way. Wasn't nobody there most of the time, and when they were, you usually wished they weren't. A home without love ain't much a home, and it gets really cold. So, I took to the streets when I was young to escape. You know, an abandoned building can be a lot warmer place than a cold home sometimes."

"How old were you? Thomas asks.

"About twelve when I started staying away."

"Twelve? How'd you survive?"

"Not sure if I really did. I just didn't stop breathing," Brian says.

"Did you have a place to stay?"

"Depends on what I was willing to do. After a while, I was willing to do a lot."

Thomas sincerely looks at him. "You've been abused?" he asks.

"I could take it. You know, I'm really just a piece of shit anyway, or so it seems."

"You don't strike me as a piece of shit. You seem better than that."

"Yea, well, pieces of shit don't get loved, and I've never been loved. Thought I was going to be one time, but...."

"But what?"

"Nothing, somethings are never meant to be," a wave of anger grows in Brian. "Even if you get close, there's always someone or something that gets in the way."

"Is that what happened to you?"

Brian looks deeply into Thomas' eyes.

"Yea, in a way," he says.

"How?" Thomas asks.

"I thought I finally found someone who gave my life meaning. I wasn't just into myself anymore, I was into her and what she cared about, and who she was. That had never happened before...and then she was gone."

"How?" Thomas asks, his voice quivering as his pain flourishes back.

"Someone came along. Took her away."

"Another guy?"

"No," Brian shakes his head. "She died."

"I'm sorry."

"Yea, I tried to save her, but I couldn't."

"You were there?"

Brain shakes his head. "No, I knew she was in trouble, and I couldn't get anyone to listen." The anger grows deeper in Brian's voice. "They should have listened."

"When did this happen? Who wouldn't listen?" Thomas asks.

Brian shakes his head as if to snap out of his thoughts.

"Hey, we're here to talk about you, not me," he exclaims.

"As you said, it's best not to struggle alone. I sense you're still going through things," Thomas replies.

"Yea, I guess I am."

Thomas turns to Brian. "We seem to have more in common than you might think."

"How's that?"

"We've both suffered great losses."

They both grow silent again for a moment.

"How did you end up at the church?" Thomas finally asks.

'I had heard of Father Isaiah and how he helped people. I was tired of the streets, and I wanted something better. So, I asked him how. How do I find something better?" Brian replies. "He said he knew, and he took me in to show me how."

"How's that been going?"

A reflective look comes over Brian.

"It's had its ups and downs, but really, enough about me. How's work going?" Brian asks.

"As usual, frustrating."

"Why?"

"I don't know, we've got some guy, and he's something. Absolutely brutal in his methods, and I can't figure out why," Thomas says with a sense of exasperation.

"Some type of revenge?" Brian says as if he's trying to help.

"Could be, but the question is why? What's happening is personal. Once I figure out the why, I might be able to figure out the who, but right now, I'm clueless."

"You have no idea?" Brian asks carefully.

"None."

A sad resignation appears on Thomas' face. The conversation goes silent once more as they look at people having fun on the ice. It's a silence that lasts until they rise to leave.

Thomas and Brian choose different directions to leave the area around the towering blue beer cans along the river. Thomas hops into his pickup truck and heads down toward Lafarge Concrete Company's dock for lake freighters. There, he turns left at the light to get on Ohio Street to head back downtown.

He's feeling thankful Brian has come into his life. He's helped lift some of the darkness that's enveloped him since that one day a couple of years ago. His thoughts soon turn to Shelly. Maybe he can start his life again, he just doesn't know, but he's strengthened by the voices telling him to live again.

Brian decides to walk back to the cathedral via the Michigan Avenue Bridge. He strides past tractor trailers waiting to get a load of cereal from the General Mills plant for deliveries throughout the Northeast. He feels like he's walking on air as he realizes he might get away with what he's doing. He sucks in the air; it's never felt so good as he descends the bridge and walks past Swannie's House, an old three-story brick bar that once served as a rooming house for sailors working on the Great Lakes.

"Yep," he says to himself. "Today is a good day!"

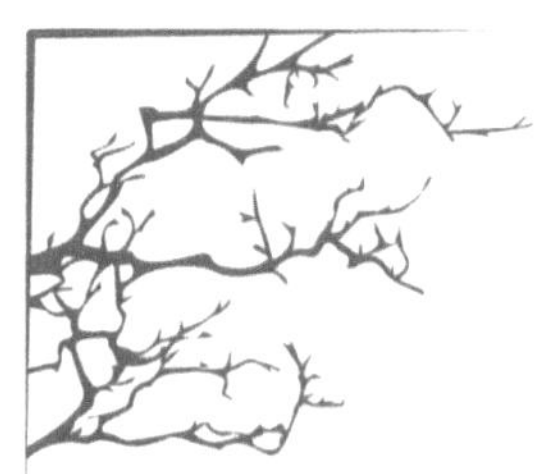

Chapter 31

Holiday music plays softly in the background as the morning sun of another new day breaks through the cracks in the drapes in Thomas' mother's room. Marcie checks the monitors. She gently pulls up the covers on the fragile woman lying on the bed and tucks in the sides to keep her warm.

Then, she takes the vial of lavender oil Thomas gave her out of her pocket and drops a pinch onto the pillow. She squeezes a seemingly lifeless hand.

"You have a good day, Mrs. Shea," she whispers.

Marcie walks briskly down the hallway as she puts on her winter coat. The shift nurse relieving her looks up when she passes the nurse's station.

"Hey, Marcie, what are you doing for the weekend?" she asks.

"I'm going to grab Tracy and Bob, and we're going to spend the day celebrating her tenth birthday by going skiing in Ellicottville and taking in some of the holiday festivities there."

"Wow, ten years."

"Sure does pass quickly," Marcie looks at her watch. "I'm running late, and you know how impatient Tracy gets."

"Don't they all at that age?"

They share a knowing smile.

"Have fun."

"Hope so," Marcie says cheerily as she heads toward the elevator.

Marcie continues her "happy to be out of work" stride across the parking ramp and to her car.

She gets in, throws her purse onto the passenger seat, and shuts the driver's door.

There's a KNOCK at her window.

She rolls down the window, and looks surprised.

"Brian, I haven't seen you in a while!"

He leans into the window as he plunges a syringe into her neck.

"I guess it's been a couple of years," he says.

"What are you doing?"

"Time of atonement."

"What?" she says.

Her body starts to fail her; she's becoming paralyzed. She's limp within moments. Only the horrifying reflection in her eyes tells Brian she's alive and aware.

A sadistic satisfying smile fills Brian's face as he opens the driver's door and pushes her over to the side.

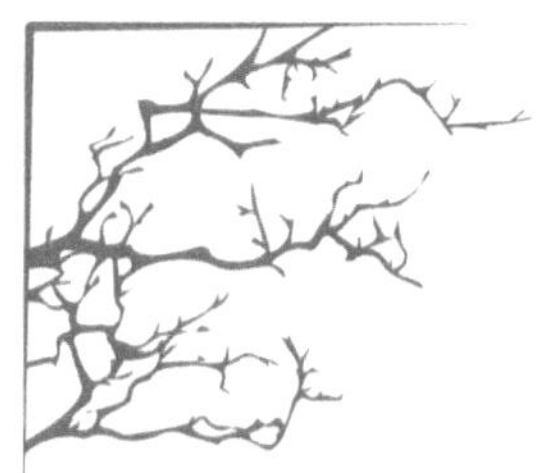

Chapter 32

For the first time in quite a while, Thomas wakes up feeling refreshed and excited. He's happy he'll be meeting Shelly for some cross-country skiing, but first, he wants to stop by the morgue to see if anything new has popped up.

When he walks into the autopsy room, he finds Ozzie standing on a step ladder as he places a jar with human kidneys on a shelf full of glass containers with other body parts. It's almost like an encyclopedic collection of human organs.

Ozzie smiles when he sees him walk in.

"Hi, Tommy. You're here early on a Saturday morning."

"I figured you'd be working. So, I decided to stop by and see how things are doing."

"These new killings are troublesome. There's a viciousness going on here I usually don't see, but I have gotten some results back from toxicology."

"What'd you find out?"

"Unfortunately, it was along the lines of what I suspected," Ozzie says as he gets down off the ladder and walks across the room. "Whoever killed them wanted them to be aware of what was happening. He, or she, used a drug called pancuronium bromide."

Thomas looks surprised. "Isn't that used during executions?"

"It is. It's used to paralyze the body but does nothing to dim the awareness of the condemned. They use other drugs for that,' Ozzie says as he moves to his desk. "Neither of our victims had a chance, and both knew it."

"Jesus. All right, well, I gotta be somewhere, but I'll stop back later."

Within a few minutes, Thomas enters Ring Road, which goes around Delaware Park in his pickup. He sees Shelly standing next to her car and checking the time on her cell phone. He pulls up and hops out.

"I wasn't sure you were going to show," She says.

"I had to make a stop."

"About the case?" She asks.

"Yea."

She studies him for a moment, she can tell by his gloomy aura it can't be good.

"Looks bad. Whatcha find out?"

"It's disappointing."

"What?"

"It's something you already know," he says, "It was just confirmed. Your ex was completely aware of what was happening to him."

The news staggers Shelly a bit, she was hoping they'd determine he was knocked out or dead already. She leans into her car to steady herself.

"I'm sorry," Thomas doesn't know if he should go and grab her or let her pull herself together. He decides to step back and let her be.

"It's not your fault," she says as she takes a moment to collect her thoughts.

Thomas nods at the meadow.

"We don't have to do this now," he says softly.

Shelly straightens up. She comes to grips with herself, like the old street warrior she is.

"No, I want to. The exercise will do me good."

"You sure?"

She looks at him. "I am,"

She begins to unload her skis from the rooftop rack on her Jeep while Thomas goes to collect his things from the back of his pickup.

In no time, they are all geared up and ready to go.

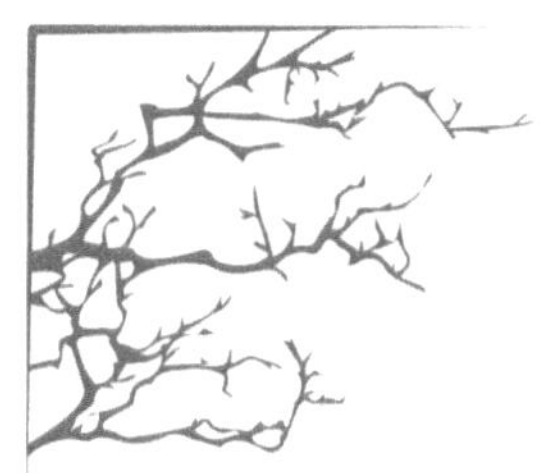

Chapter 33

Tracy sadly sits looking out the window at cars passing by. She has a cell phone to her ear. She yells out to her dad in another part of the house.

"Dad, mom's late again, and she's not answering the phone."

Her father shouts back from the kitchen.

"Don't worry, she'll be here."

"But it's my birthday weekend."

Her dad walks in while drying his hands with a kitchen towel.

"Give her time. She has an important job that sometimes makes her late. You know that."

"But she promised."

"Has she ever broken a promise to you?"

"No."

"Okay, then, give her a few more minutes. You want to help me finish the dishes."

"Not really."

He expected that answer. He goes back into the kitchen while Tracy dials Marcie's number yet again.

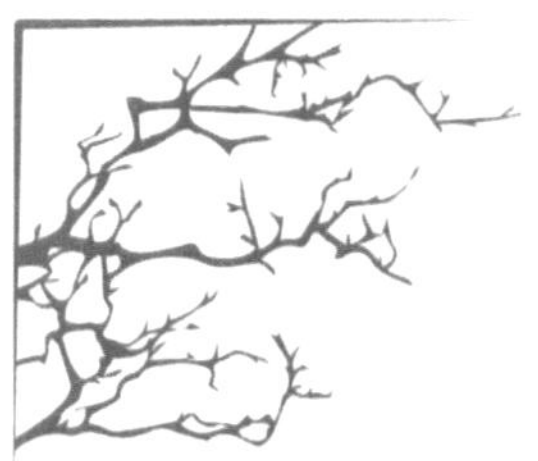

Chapter 34

Thomas steadies himself on the cross-country skis as he comes to a small slope going down to the meadow area.

"Remember, I haven't done this for a long time," he says to Shelly.

"Don't worry. I won't let you fall too far behind."

"Just don't let me fall, period. My body's getting old."

Shelly smiles and looks him up and down.

"Doesn't look like too old to me."

"That's only because you're not in it."

They share a laugh. Shelly moves to the crest of the slope. She looks at Thomas.

"You ready?"

"As ready as I'll ever be."

She slips down the slope and starts laying tracks over pearly white snow covering the vast expanse of the meadow area. A meadow that also serves as a golf course during the warmer months. Thomas glides into the tracks and follows behind her.

They ski along the rolling hills of the meadow through snow-covered pine trees and the trail leading across the stone bridge going over Delaware Avenue. Sounds of tires spinning across wet streets fill the air as they cross over. They make their way past hearty souls playing tennis on the snow-cleared courts and turn left down a street filled with stately homes.

The path continues until it goes down a ridge to the barren Japanese Garden near the base of the Greek Revival-styled Buffalo and Erie County Historical Building. One of the few remaining buildings from the 1901 Pan-American Exposition which was the first World's

Fair to use electric lights and where President William McKinley, the 25th President of the United States, was assassinated.

The tip of his skis comes to a stop by a frozen pond surrounding a small island sticking out of the ice a few feet from shore. Thomas breathes in the air. It's been a long time since he has felt so good. His heart is pumping rapidly, oxygen courses through his body, and he suddenly becomes aware of how attractive Shelly really is. A beauty he noticed before but now feels it.

Shelly glides in next to him.

"You're doing good," she says.

Thomas laughs. "Sheer determination. I'll be damned if I'll look bad in front of you."

She leans in close to him.

"Actually, you're looking pretty good to me."

"Am I?"

"Yea."

She leans in closer and gently kisses his lips.

He kisses her back.

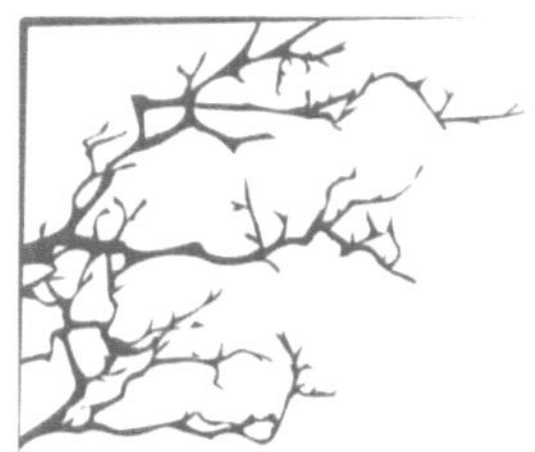

Chapter 35

A naked Marcie lies paralyzed on a stainless steel cutting table. Brian can see the sheer horror in her eyes as she looks at the meat hooks hanging from the ceiling.

He sorts his surgical knives like he's re-enacting some scene from Dexter, the show about a serial killer mutilating other serial killers.

"You're probably wondering if someone is going to help you," Brian says to a speechless Marcie. "In the back of my mind, I keep wondering about that myself."

He checks the blade on one of the knives, it's perfect. He moves to the table Marcie is stretched out on and looks down at her.

"I was thinking the same thing with Teddy when I dumped his body into the lake It was kind of fun. I took his head and hurled it like a discus across the water!"

Brian slides the surgical knife down Marcie's motionless thigh. Blood oozes out from the narrow wound it creates.

Brian studies the knife.

"This one slices nice," he states. "What do you think?"

Her terror-filled eyes scream at him. Brian continues on as if he doesn't notice.

"Now Troy, that was a bit more gruesome. Creative, I thought, but gruesome. Have you ever seen a man fed into a large wood chipper? It's extremely messy."

Brian cuts another wound down her thigh next to the original one.

"Surreal would be a good word for that."

As he cuts another slice, tears fall out of the corners of her eyes.

Now you," he says to Marcie, "I've had time to think about that. How best for you to meet your end."

He draws the blade down her thigh again. Blood floods the table.

He leans in close to her face.

"I thought, why not stroll down memory lane for this one."

Brian's eyes are inches away from hers.

"You remember, don't you? I know you do."

He leans back up. Moves to the other thigh and slices a groove in it.

"Oh, well, time to stop talking and get working. I have to get back to the cathedral before the father starts wondering where I've been and starts questioning me – again. "

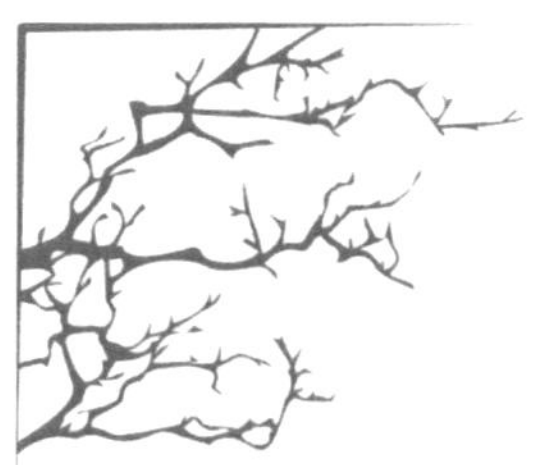

Chapter 36

The kiss by the frozen pond at the Japanese Garden set in motion a series of events that led Thomas and Shelly back to her house to start a fire in the stone-faced fireplace in the living room. The serene day with bright sunshine has turned into a raging snowstorm filled with blowing winds and growing snow mounds as night falls.

Thomas lays naked on the floor with his back against a couch. He's covered by a warm comforter. Shelly comes in wearing only a long T-shirt and carrying two cups of steaming hot chocolate.

She plops down next to him; she's flying high on life as she hands him one of the cups.

"My own special recipe."

"What's that?"

She coyly peers at him over the lip of her cup. Her voice becomes sultry, seductive.

"Secret. Try a sip."

Thomas takes a sip.

"Good," he says.

"Told you."

He smacks his lips a little.

"I taste a bit of butterscotch," he surmises.

"Close. Caramel with a dash of coconut oil."

"I thought it was a secret?"

"Now it's our secret," she says as she leans in close to give him another kiss.

A long loving kiss.

"Hey, I've gotta question," Thomas says.

"What"

"You said back at the morgue that you'd been through the process of identifying someone. Why?"

She takes a breath before looking deeply into his eyes. "There was a time when I lived much differently than I do now. I had more of a street existence. Did things just to survive. Quite a few of the people I spent most of my time around left us too soon. Often with no family or at least a family that cared about whether they lived or died. We buried a couple of 'em."

"We?"

"Me, and some of the other girls I used to dance with."

"Dance?" The question hangs in the air for a second.

"I used to work at Flay's and the Kit-Kat Club," she confesses.

"What did you do?"

"Like I said, danced."

Thomas knows all about these places. They're dive bar strip clubs where heavy-duty people with bad attitudes hang out. A lot of cases he worked on originated in those clubs and spilled out elsewhere. It's a place you gotta be tough to survive.

"I hope I don't disappoint you?"

He smiles and slowly shakes his head.

"No, you don't. I get how life can be. The roads we end up traveling sometimes."

A tear comes to her eye as she folds herself into Thomas' chest. She feels herself letting herself go a little more.

Thomas can tell he's slipping away into her, too. Something he hasn't experienced in so very long - the love of a woman who stirs his emotions.

Suddenly, feelings of guilt grow in him. He really shouldn't be able to live like this when the ones he loved can't anymore.

Shelly senses a struggle going on in Thomas. She notices the passion draining from his lips. A fear instantly rises in her. Was it a mistake to tell him about her past, even a little?

"You do hate me now, don't you?" she asks nervously.

The sound of her voice breaking catches Thomas by surprise.

"No," he shakes his head and produces another soft smile. "But I'm not sure if I can do this." Tears well up in his eyes. "I just feel so guilty."

She holds his face in her hands and stares into the pain in his eyes. He just stares back at her as the image of his wife and daughter at the cemetery urging him to live plays out again and again in his head.

But as he looks into Shelly's eyes, he can feel his emotions calming. Something is beginning to change in him. Something grand.

"Are you okay?" she asks.

"Not sure. Maybe."

Thomas pulls Shelly closer and tighter as she gently plays with the hair on his chest. The flames roar higher in the fireplace as they embrace.

Later, as smoldering ashes rise from the fireplace, Thomas and Shelly lie asleep while intertwined in each other arms under the warm comforter. His cell phone vibrates somewhere in the room. It jolts Thomas awake from his sleep.

He searches around until he finds it under his shirt on the floor.

Thomas groggily speaks into the phone as Shelly opens her eyes.

"Shea, here."

He listens.

"Okay, where?"

He hangs up the phone and turns to Shelly.

"I'm sorry, but duty calls."

He gets up, puts on his shirt and pants. Shelly leans onto her side, the comforter up over her chest.

"Coming back?" she asks.

Thomas buckles up his pants.

"You want me back?"

Shelly smiles.

"I do."

Thomas smiles back as he puts his socks and shoes on. He's feeling a burst of happiness.

"Then I'll be back."

Thomas puts on his coat and heads out. Shelly puts her head back down on a pillow. She's feeling a burst of happiness, too. It's been a long time for her as well.

Before long, Thomas pulls up to see a crowd of people standing behind yellow police tape cordoning off the area around the Black Rock Prison for Women's flagpole. They're staring up at a partially mutilated and dismembered body. All the organs and legs are gone. The lower half of the remains are layers of skin cut into strips. It flutters in the wind like a flag.

Thomas looks around at the sea of first responders standing there looking up in disbelief. Kayla is among them.

Thomas slowly walks into the crowd. The closer he gets, the more he realizes he recognizes the face on the body.

Then it hits and anger fills his eyes. What flutters in the wind are what's left of Marcie. He growls at no one in particular.

"Get her down," he demands.

A crime scene technician hears him.

"We can't until we collect the evidence."

"The evidence will be there after she comes down."

Fire burns from Thomas' eyes. Now is not the time for anyone to challenge him - and that means anyone.

"I said to get her down," he growls.

Kayla steps in between Thomas and the technician.

"Thomas, we've got to collect evidence first. Look at the shoe prints around the bottom of the flagpole. Look familiar?"

Thomas studies the prints, they have similar markings to the ones taken at the waterfront and Chestnut Ridge scenes.

"I don't want her up there in front of everyone, Kayla. She needs to come down!"

"Okay, okay, just let us get some things done quickly, and then we'll get her down. Okay?"

Thomas knows she's right. But looking at Marcie's face, Thomas finds it hard to handle all the thoughts running through his mind. Her kindness, gentle smiles and ways, and her lovely daughter. One thought after another bombards his brain so much it hurts.

The technician quickly isolates a couple of shoe prints on the ground using sticks and yellow tape for imaging and casting work after the body is removed. Then she checks the pole for finger or hand prints - there aren't any.

"We're ready," she says to Thomas. "We just have to be careful not to step in the area I've marked off."

Thomas motions for several firefighters to come over, untie the rope, and lower what's left of Marcie's body to the ground. A hospital gurney is brought in to accept her remains. Thomas covers what's left of her body with a white sheet.

Then, he examines her neck. There, behind her left ear, he finds a puncture wound.

He calls Kayla over.

"I think we need to check to see if Marcie worked here," he says as he nods toward the front doors of the prison.

Thomas pulls the sheet over Marcie's head. He looks out on the road and sees the morgue wagon pulling in. He glances over at Kayla, pain as sadness drips from his eyes.

"She's got a young daughter."

Tracy still sits on the couch staring out the window. Only now, her clothes are wrinkled, and her hair is all messed up from staying here all night long.

She stopped trying to call her mom on the phone hours ago.

She watches as Thomas and Kayla pull up in his pickup truck. Her eyes lock onto them as they exit the vehicle. She stumbles off the couch as the doorbell rings.

Slowly she opens the front door. Fear grows in her belly, even worse than what was there already.

She looks up at Thomas.

"I know you," she says to him.

"Hi, Tracy. Is your dad home?"

A coldness fills Tracy's soul. She senses her world is about to fall in.

"Do you know where my mommy is?"

Thomas hesitates; he's tormented.

"Yes, honey, I do."

Tracy's voice cracks. "Where?"

Thomas finds himself fighting back tears. He knows he has to keep strong, but as he looks into this little girl's face, he's not sure if he can.

"I need your dad, Tracy"

"Where is she?"

Thomas bends down.

"Please, Tracy, can you get your dad?"

Bob appears at the door, he looks as disheveled as Tracy. Sleep escaped him last night, too.

"Hello, can I help you?"

Tracy looks up at her dad.

"Daddy, this is the man mommy talks about who sits with his mom."

Bob looks at Thomas, it takes a second for it to sink in.

"You work homicide, don't you?"

"Yes, I do. This is my partner, Detective Kayla Harrison."

"If you're looking for Marcie, we're not sure where she is. We've tried to report her missing, but not enough time has passed, I guess."

"They know," Tracy says.

"You do?" Bob asks.

Thomas takes a deep breath.

"Unfortunately."

Now Bob starts to shake and break down.

"Oh, God," he says as he grabs Tracy.

"Dad?" she cries as she falls into her father's arms. Her fear freely flows out now.

Thomas and Kayla turn away as they fight back their own tears.

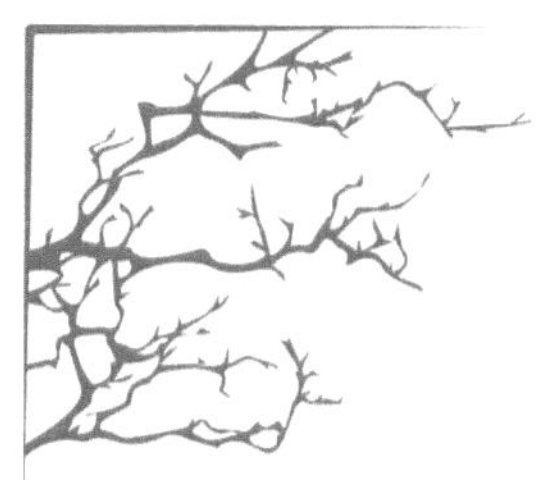

Chapter 37

Chris leans back in his chair at bar in Shane's while checking out the betting odds on the upcoming Buffalo Sabres' game on his smartphone when the front door opening grabs his attention. A streak of daylight shines across the floor. In strolls Brian, stopping almost immediately while his eyes adjust to the darkness after walking in from the bright sun.

Chris notices Brian struggling to see.

"Sunny day," he says.

"Yea, can't see a thing," Brian responds.

"Give it a second. What can I do for you?"

"Looking for a friend."

"Only one person here," he nods toward a back corner, "and he's over there."

"Thanks," Brian says as his sight comes back enough to walk across the room to the back corner where Thomas sits hunkered down over his drink. He sadly stares into a glass of Old Granddad on the rocks while swirling it around slowly. Brian walks up to the table.

"They burned to death," Thomas says without looking up.

The statement catches Brian off guard.

"Who?"

Tears well up in Thomas' eyes.

"My wife...daughter."

Brian is stunned, he wasn't expecting this type of news. He slowly sits down in the chair across the table from Thomas.

"What happened?"

"Car accident."

"How?"

"Does it matter?"

"No, I guess not."

Thomas continues to swirl the drink in his hand as he watches the cubes swirl around in the caramel-colored liquid.

Brian nods at the glass.

"How many have you had?" he asks.

"You're looking at it."

"So I'm not too late."

"In a manner of speaking."

Brian watches as Thomas continues to stare into his swirling drink. "Do you really think there are any more answers to be found in there?" he says to Thomas.

"Not looking for answers."

"What are you looking for?"

"Escape. That's why I always end up here."

"Is this where you want to be?"

Thomas looks up. His eyes pierce through Brian's.

"I never wanted to be here," he says.

"Then why don't you go somewhere else?"

Thomas looks around the dark empty bar in the middle of the day. The rays of sunshine coming though the window struggle to get through the smoke-stained glass.

"This is where I should be."

"Sitting alone in a run-down bar in the dark?"

"Feels right."

"How steep of a price do you want to pay for something that wasn't your fault? Something you couldn't even control?" Brian asks him.

"Until I can forget," Thomas says as he looks back down into his drink.

"You never will."

"I know."

"Why not choose a different path?" Brian challenges him.

"I never chose this one."

"But you've decided to stay on it."

"We do what comes naturally."

"This isn't natural. This is a living death."

"Death. Now that's something. That's what I'm supposed to do, figure out death. Like, why'd your mom get killed in such a horrendous way? Sometimes I don't have a fucking clue!" A rage builds in Thomas. "I've got a guy who killed the woman who has been looking after my mom for the past six months as she rots away in a bed. She was an angel"

"Your mom?" Brian feels like the hits just keep on coming since he walked in the door.

"Yea, a nurse. She worked at the Garden Gate Assisted Living Center. Somebody mutilated her yesterday and hung her remains on a flagpole outside Black Rock Prison during the night. She was a beautiful woman in many ways and a mom to a wonderful young daughter. A young daughter who'll never be the same after what I told her today. Yea, I gotta great fucking job and life."

Brian feels his stomach tighten a little as he tries to stay focused on his mission here.

"Sometimes, it's not for you to figure out," he says, hopeful he never does.

"That's my job, figuring it out. And I don't have a fucking clue."

Hearing this little bit of news always makes Brian feel a little better.

"Maybe you should relax and not think about it," he says to Thomas, "but put the drink down. That's something you don't need."

Thomas stares into the swirling golden liquid, he knows Brian is right. Just like he knows the reason he called Brian in the first place was to get him to talk him out of having that first drink. The first drink that will lead to others, usually many others.

Thomas places the drink on the table and pushes it away.

"Let's go take a walk around the waterfront. There's a holiday festival down at Canalside; it might help you feel better," Brian says as he looks down at Thomas.

"All right," Thomas agrees as he rises. The invitation excites him as he seeks ways not to drink, even if he's carrying a heavy heart.

They both head for the door. Chris calls out.

"Hey, Detective, you have a good day."

Thomas stops and they exchange a deep personal look as if they were saying goodbye to each other...maybe forever.

"You, too, Chris."

Thomas and Brian walk out of the darkness and into the bright winter sunshine.

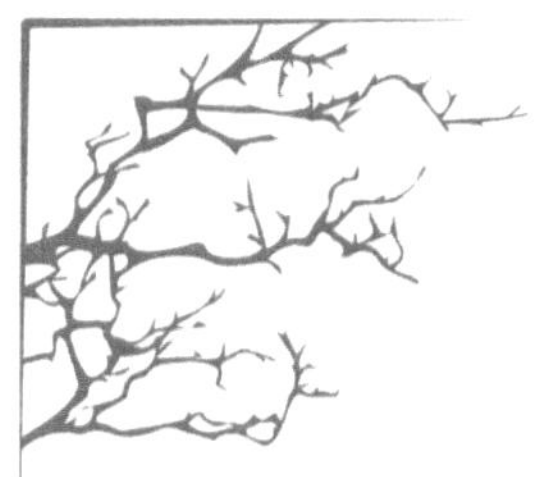

Chapter 38

Kayla sits behind a stack of files when Thomas walks into the squad room. She studies him closely as he makes his way across the floor and takes a seat at his desk.

"You okay?" she asks him.

Thomas slowly nods his head.

"Yea."

"Where'd you end up going yesterday?"

"Shane's."

Kayla sighs. Thomas notices her slightly shaking her head.

"I didn't have a drink," he deadpans.

"No?"

"Didn't seem to be the right thing to do. I called a friend. We ended up at Canalside. They've done quite a job rejuvenating that area."

"Definitely looks better than the big hole that was left after the Aud came down."

"It does. It was a good time. Exactly what I needed."

"Yea, yesterday morning was rough," Kayla says as she reflects on the tortuous look that appeared on that young girl's face. "I don't know if I'm going to be able to do that again."

"It's part of the job, Kayla," Thomas says sympathetically. "If you're going to work homicide, you're going to see and experience a lot of heartaches. Both yours and someone else's, but that heartache makes me more determined to catch those who caused it. We can't let them run free forever, and there can be a lot of satisfaction in being the one who stops and catches them. There is a good side here."

Pain flows out of Kayla's eyes as she looks into Thomas'.

As she starts to say something, Superintendent Trowbridge strides into the room and announces, "I think I have some information for you." He's carrying a large manila envelope.

"What might that be?" Thomas asks.

"You were right, the nurse worked at the prison. The scene yesterday outside the prison shook people up. They started talking about when all three worked there and what happened one night on the psychiatric ward," Trowbridge explains.

The statement piques Thomas' curiosity, "What happened?"

"May I sit down?"

Thomas swings a wooden chair around so Trowbridge can sit.

"I found out about an incident that happened about two and a half years ago. A young woman, Jennifer Irving, was brutally attacked and murdered by another inmate. Apparently, all three of your victims worked on that ward at the time this happened."

Trowbridge hands the manila envelope he's been carrying to Thomas.

"The photos are rather gruesome," he says as Thomas takes the envelope.

Thomas opens the envelope and pulls out several photos. He studies the images of a young woman who's been mutilated beyond recognition.

"A woman snapped and secretly locked herself in a storage closet with this young woman and did indescribable things to her," Trowbridge adds. "Including slicing off slabs of her skin which she fed into a meat grinder she had stolen and stored in the closet. The finishing touch was decapitation."

"How come you didn't mention this before?" Thomas asks.

"Didn't know about it. Everything was kept extremely quiet and confidential. I didn't know about it until today when loose tongues started wagging."

Thomas hands the photos to Kayla.

"From the looks of things, I'd say we might have our connection," he says.

Kayla stares in disbelief at what she's holding.

"Is there a log of others who worked on the floor when this happened?"

"I'm sure there is," Trowbridge replies. "I'd have to put in a document request to get it out of storage."

"Can you do that?" Thomas asks him.

"Yes."

"Good. Can it get rushed?"

"I think so."

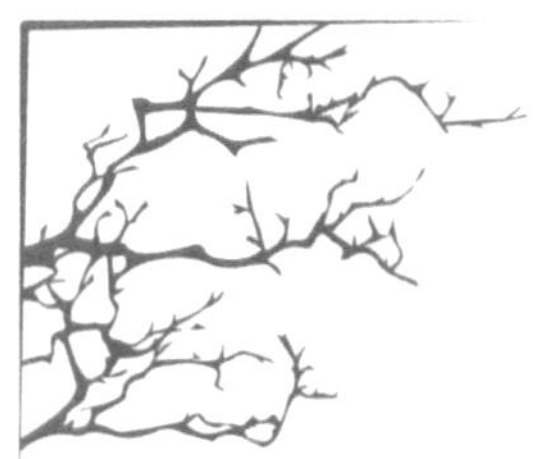

Chapter 39

Brian moves slowly through the shadows along the wall aisle in the cathedral. He walks with his head bowed and his hands clasped in front of him as though he's walking towards his executioner. He thinks about what Thomas said about Marcie.

He's never thought about how what he was doing would affect others. Actually, he never has. Even when he was young. He could hurt someone and see their mother, wife, sister, or daughter the next day; he'd tell her how sorry he was for what happened to her son, brother, father, or husband - depending on who Brian visited with ill intent.

He could do it because he didn't care and was devoid of real emotions. He didn't care about life, living, or himself. Living was a burden that made him angry. Then he found Jennifer. He remembers the first time he saw her standing quietly off to the side with her brownish hair softly laying across her shoulders.

When he looked into her soft brown eyes, he knew his life had instantly changed. He felt love. Pure love. He knew everything would never be the same. He just didn't know it would get worse.

Brian reaches the Statue of the Virgin Mary and the table full of candles at her feet. He reaches for a lighting stick. His hand shakes as he lights the stick from the flame of a burning candle.

His shaking makes it difficult to light another candle. Finally, a small flame flickers on one, and Brian blows out the burning lighting stick.

He lowers himself to his knees and rests his head against his folded hands. He begins to weep.

The tears come slowly at first, but soon his chest heaves as he starts to cry uncontrollably. His cries echo throughout the cathedral.

Brian looks up at the Virgin Mary, tears streaming from his eyes, then he buries his head in his hands again.

Father Isaiah emerges from the shadows.

"Brian, what's going on?" Father Isaiah asks in an accusatory tone.

Startled and caught off-guard, Brian jumps up. He grabs the handle of the sheathed knife stuck in his belt under his shirt.

"I think we need to talk," Father Isaiah demands.

"Not now, Father. Please," Brian begs. "Now is not a good time."

"I think now is exactly the right time."

He grabs Brian by the arm and starts to force him to go the way he wants. Brian snatches his arm back.

"Father, now is not the time!"

"I've talked to the Bishop about you. I want to know what's going on!"

He grabs Brian's arm again. A panic rises in Brian. He doesn't know what to do. All he wants is a moment to collect his thoughts, and this guy won't give it to him.

The whole thing makes Brian's nerves raw. Too raw to think right.

In a flash, Brian's thumb expertly dislodges the strap on the sheath holding the knife under his shirt. He takes it out and plunges it up under Father Isaiah's rib cage until the tip ruptures his heart. Brian's surprised at how easy the movements came. Too easy, he thinks.

Watching Father Isaiah fall to the floor as blood floods out from his gut unleashes a torrent of mixed emotions and thoughts in Brian. He knows he has to do something, and he has to do it quickly, before anyone enters into the cathedral from the cold outdoors.

He runs across the altar and through the vestry into the rectory. Running into Father Isaiah's bathroom, he rips the shower curtain from its rings and hurries back to his side.

Laying the curtain down alongside the now lifeless body of Father Isaiah, Brian gets on the opposite side of the body and flips it onto the curtain. This causes more blood to flow out of the wound. The blood flows everywhere across the curtain and floor.

Brian stands back and thinks for a moment. What the hell is he going to do now? He doesn't want to drag the body. That will just move the blood all over the place. He learned that when he pulled Casey's body across the floor inside the grain elevator.

He needs to control the blood. But how?

Then it dawns on him. There are large totes used for garbage out back by the kitchen. A couple of them should be empty. He darts back across the altar and winds his way to the kitchen's back door. Rushing outside, he grabs a tote and rolls it back to where Father Isaiah's body lies.

The top of the tote flips open as Brian lays it down on the floor. He positions it so he can slide the body and curtain inside of it as much as he can. He then flips the tote up to drop everything in. He takes the tote back out through the kitchen door and sets it tp the side.

Now, he has to remove the blood from the cathedral floor. There's a mop and bucket in the corner of the kitchen. He fills it with water, detergent, and plenty of bleach. Then, he hurries back out to the blood-stained floor; he's thankful that nobody comes in while he cleans up the mess.

Now, he thinks, one last thing to do. Get rid of the body, but how?

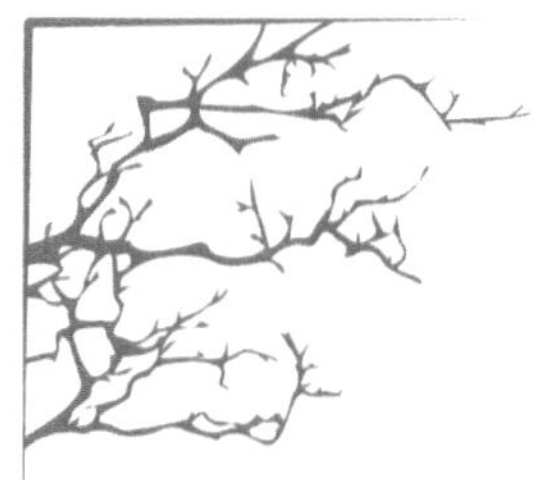

Chapter 40

Thomas and Kayla each work through stacks of files on their desks; completely unaware that on the other side of the magnificent edifice outside their window, Brian is wheeling the large tote down a snow-covered sidewalk toward the railroad tunnels near the cathedral.

"Okay, so what do we know?" Thomas asks, partially to himself and partially to Kayla.

Kayla reads a file.

"They all worked at the prison, all left about the same time, and we know two of them underwent some level of personality change. And it might be related to the killing and mutilation of that young woman. Did the nurse change at all that you know of?" she replies.

"Haven't known her that long or that close. We'll have to ask the husband."

"That'll be a nice conversation, I'm sure," Kayla says sadly.

"Yea," a look of pending regret crosses his face.

"Well, we know they were all killed, at least in some ways, as the young woman in the photos," Kayla notes as she gets back to business. "So, I say we follow this to see where it takes us."

Thomas nods in agreement.

"I've read the report on the young woman," he says. "She was 26, worked as a drug mule, and was extremely bipolar. She could be upbeat and emotional one minute and meek as a lamb who crawled into herself the next. Haven't seen anything that would have caused her to be a target for what happened."

"Victim of opportunity?"

"Could be. No revenge motive that the investigators knew of. Violent and mentally unstable people can create worlds where innocent and unsuspecting people play roles. Sometimes, the role is that of a threat that has to be eliminated, at least in their minds."

He sets a file down.

"Unfortunately, or maybe, fortunately," he continues, "the nutcase killed herself a couple of days after she did her deed."

"But why kill people who worked on the ward at the time this girl was killed?"

Thomas shakes his head at that question.

"Damn, if I know," he says, "this girl was homeless at 14, she was surviving as a hooker by 16, and was a convicted drug smuggler at 22. If there's one constant running through the story of her short life is that she never had anyone who really cared or tried to protect her at all. So, I can't see anyone caring enough about her for her death to be involved here, but that doesn't mean I haven't missed seeing something," he leans back, "It sure does seem like it is somehow. I, mean, it makes sense even if it doesn't."

Thomas rubs his eyes; he's getting kind of wiped out for the night.

"That's enough for the night. We really can't do anything more until we get the listing of other personnel who worked in the psych ward. Hopefully, everything will stay quiet until we do," Thomas says as he rises and puts on his coat.

Kayla puts her files down. She's ready for a drink, actually.

"Where are you going to go?" she asks.

"Don't know, someplace where I can just think."

Kayla puts on her coat, too.

"Want me to wake you in the morning?"

Thomas smiles at her as they walk out of the office.

"You know, I think I'll be okay," he says.

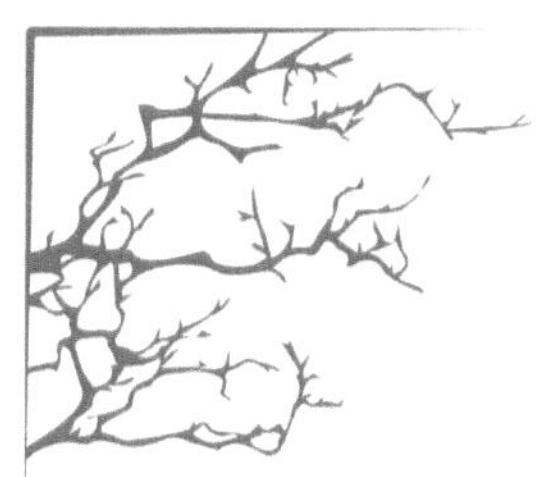

Chapter 41

Brian frantically pulls the tote carrying Father Isaiah's body down a slopping icy sidewalk that leads to the railroad tracks behind the cathedral.

He slips and slides as he struggles to keep the tote from tipping over as he rolls it up and over a snow mound and onto the tracks.

Once he gets the tote on the tracks, he pulls it into the tunnel where there isn't any snow. The one thing he doesn't notice as the tote wheels pound against the wood ties is the homeless man scurrying off into the darkness to escape detection. The man huddles in a crevice as he watches Brian's silhouette come to a stop.

Brian tips the tote over and pulls the body out of it. He places Father Isaiah's head on one rail and his upper thighs over the other rail until he's completely stretched across the tracks. This way, when a train comes, he thinks, it will mutilate the body and possibly disguise the knife wound. After he's satisfied he's laid out the body just the way he wants it, Brian grabs the tote and wheels it out of the tunnel, and goes back up to the rectory.

His mind reels as he walks. Thoughts shout at him inside his head: This should not be happening; It's just not part of the plan; The father wasn't supposed to die; He never did anything wrong to me! He just tried to give me a new and better life. A life I've just thrown into the river!

The thoughts turns his stomach. A fire burns in his head with every heartbeat. He runs into some bushes and heaves his guts out. Sweat pours from his face and forehead. What the hell have I done? he screams to himself.

Then a different sort of panic rises in him. What if he can't finish his mission? It's all he has left that give his life some purpose. He's got to finish. He knows what he has to do. He just has to be quicker about it now to make sure he gets it done.

Yep, that's what he has to do. Speed up the timetable.

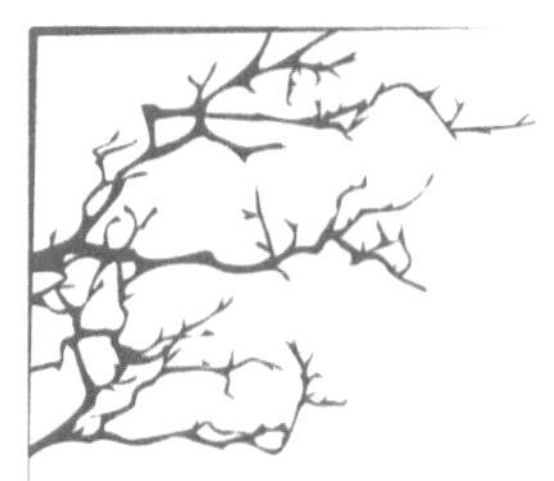

Chapter 42

Back in the train tunnel, the homeless man sneaks over to the body after he's sure Brian is gone and won't come back. He uses a match to light up the body's face. The homeless man recognizes Father Isaiah and starts to cry as he recognizes the face of one of the only people in the area who treated the homeless man as if he was someone; As if he really counted even though he lived in a confined world of solitude, darkness, and dirt.

Grabbing the body by the ankles, the homeless man uses every ounce of energy his malnourished body can muster to pull Father Isaiah's remains off of the tracks. He places it against the wall of the tunnel. Then he sits down next to the body and puts its head on his lap. He strokes Father Isaiah's hair as the tears rain down his cheeks. He stares into the dead man's face as he remembers the nights Father Isaiah would quietly make his way to the tunnels with warm bedding and food for the souls stranded there. He never made a show of it. He just did what he had to do to remain true to his faith and do what he thought was right and needed.

The homeless man stays with the body long enough for it stiffen up and turn cold and blue before he decides to let it go. Then he gently rests it against the wall, gets up, and walks out of the tunnel into the full light of day.

He walks past the back part of the cathedral and around the corner to police headquarters. He steps inside and makes his way to the front desk.

Within seconds, a full response by police fire, and EMS head to the train tunnel.

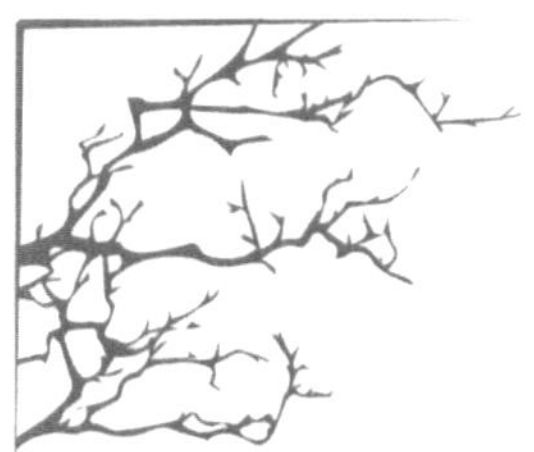

Chapter 43

Thomas sits in his mother's room while staring at the falling snow outside the window. There's a small pile of garbage from a take-out meal on the plastic hospital table next to him. The squeaky wheels of a rolling cart comes to a stop in the corridor just outside the room.

A nurse's aide enters. Thomas studies her; tries to smile. She moves quickly as she grabs the small garbage can by the bed. Then she spies the garbage on the plastic table.

Thomas notices and starts to clean it up.

"I'm sorry," he says quietly.

"That's all right," she smiles warmly, "I can get it."

"No, it's not your job to clean up after me."

Thomas gathers everything up and places it in the garbage can she's holding in her hands. A look of appreciation comes over her face.

"Thank you!"

"Thank you for looking out for my mom." The words hit him like a gut punch. He said the same words to Marcie just a few days ago.

"You're welcome," she says with a sweet young voice.

Thomas quietly watches as she replaces the full bag with an empty one in the can and leaves.

The sound of the squeaky wheel fades as she pushes the cart down the hallway.

About an hour or so later, Thomas is wrapped up in his coat to keep warm while resting on the chair. He slowly becomes aware of a voice trying to speak over the sounds of the machines beeping and humming. It's instantly familiar

He moves to the side of the bed and takes the mask off his mom's face; peers lovingly into her eyes.

"Mom, you're back!"

After he alerts the night staff to her awakening, Thomas sits in amazement watching his mother sip ice water from a little straw. Her voice might be raspy, but it's the most beautiful sound he's heard in a long time.

His heart sinks when the phone in his pocket starts to vibrate.

The phone keeps on vibrating, and then it stops, then it starts, stops, and starts again.

He reaches into his pocket and puts it to his ear.

"Shea here," he says disappointingly.

Kayla's on the other end.

"We've got another. In the train tunnel by headquarters." He hears her voice say.

Thomas instantly sounds resigned, "Okay, be there in twenty."

Thomas regretfully hangs up the phone and slides it back into his pocket. He looks adoringly at his mother.

"Hey, Mom, I've gotta go for a little while, but I'll be back."

She reaches up and weakly strokes his face. She struggles to speak.

"I love you," she forces out.

"I love you, too."

As Thomas steps out in the hallway, the attending physician motions him over to the nurse's station.

"We all loved Marcie. She made this place better when she got here a couple of years ago. I hope you find whoever did that to her," the doctor says. "I also know she was the one who kept you updated on your mother's condition."

"Yes, she did," Thomas sadly replies.

"I want you to know what's going on. Her brain activity is peaking, and that's why she's awake right now, but it won't last."

"How long?"

"Probably not more than a few days. A week at most...possibly."

"And then she fades away again?"

"Actually, Detective, this type of activity, when it happens in advanced cases like this, typically signals the end of her life's journey."

"So, she dies?"

"Usually, I'm sorry," the doctor says as comforting as he can.

Thomas shakes his head knowingly as he walks toward the elevator. He really doesn't like whomever this killer is. As a matter of fact, the killer taking precious time away from his mother is really pissing him off.

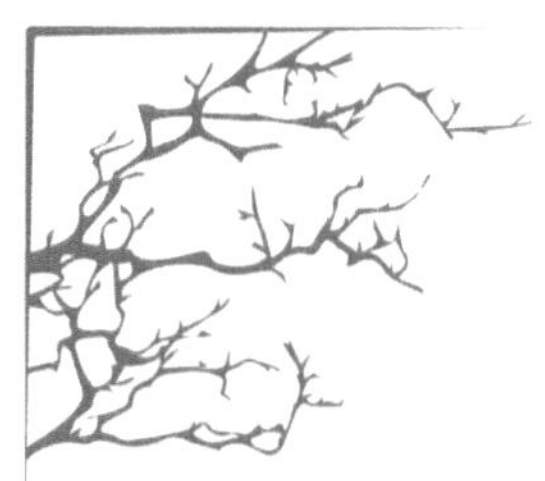

Chapter 44

The tracks have been shut down, and police have flood lights up and running, when Thomas comes walking down the tracks. Kayla walks out of the bright lights to greet Thomas.

"We've found the body of Father Isaiah," she says sadly.

"Ah, no," Thomas responds, his voice flat. "How'd we find the body?"

"One of the homeless guys living in the tunnels saw the body get dumped. He came into headquarters and reported it."

"What did he see?"

"Not much. A man pulled the body in here inside a garbage tote. He tipped it over, pulled the body out, and placed it on the tracks. The homeless guy said he pulled it

off the tracks after the man left. It was then he realized who had been killed. The guy's in bad shape, in more ways than one."

"Where is he?"

"At the station, he doesn't know any more than what he's already told us."

Thomas looks around at the activities going on. There's nothing left for him to do here. He walks out of the tunnel and looks around at the snow near the entrance. He spots the two-wheel tracks of the tote in the snow.

He looks at the tracks. They go across the street and up an unshoveled sidewalk on the other side. He walks across the street and follows the tracks up to the rectory of the cathedral.

The tracks stop at a wooden fenced area. Thomas opens the gate to find several garbage totes neatly lined up together. Except for one facing backward in a corner.

Thomas steps into the fenced-in area and pulls the tote out. He spins it around. There's blood all down the front. He steps back out so he doesn't touch anything else and gets on his phone.

Kayla answers her phone.

"Harrison."

"Kayla, Thomas, get a crime scene crew up to the rectory. I believe I've found the tote used to move Father Isaiah's body."

"Will do."

"Oh, and Kayla, there are shoe prints along the wheel tracks of the tote on the sidewalk. They seem completely isolated from any other prints. Make sure a technician takes images and casts of them."

"That's clear," Kayla responds. "We're sending a crime scene crew up to you now. We've also sent additional backup."

"Okay," Thomas hangs up as he looks around. He walks to the back door and tries the handle. It's locked. As backup arrives, he rings the doorbell and knocks on the door. Nothing.

As an officer walks up to him, Thomas motions for him to follow.

"Let's see if we can get into the rectory through the cathedral," he says.

The officer follows Thomas around to the front and through the cathedral and vestry to the door of the rectory. Thomas tries the handle. It's locked as well.

"Okay, well, we're going to need to get a search warrant. I guess this might have to wait," he says while wishing he could just go in like he did at the grain elevator.

The officer follows Thomas back out. He stops as the smell of bleach strikes him. . He knows that smell is not always a good sign.

He follows his nose to where the smell is the strongest. As Thomas studies the floor, he notices white stains in front of the statue of Mary.

He bends down and rubs his finger in it. Then he dabs his finger against his tongue to get a taste. It's salty, as he expected.

"Chlorine bleach was used here recently," he says.

"How do you know?" the officer asks incredulously.

"I think this white chalky substance is caused by bleach breaking down into its parts after it dries. One of those parts is salt, and salt leaves a white residue if the bleach hasn't been properly mopped up. Also, bleach is used to remove blood stains. So. we need to test this entire area for blood to see if some got away," Thomas says to the officer as he rises. "Stay here and make sure nothing gets disturbed before they can do their tests."

"Yes, sir," the officer replies.

Thomas walks out into the growing darkness of night as the officer assumes his post.

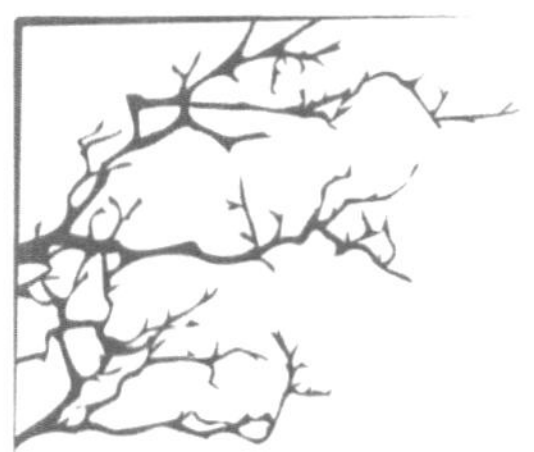

Chapter 45

Brian is startled by the sound of Thomas' pickup truck coming to a stop on the wet street in front of Shelly's house. He's been watching her through a side window covered with bushes as he gets ready to make his move. He sinks further into the bushes to hide from Thomas. He's not quite sure why Thomas has come here, but he knows he can't step out now and do what he was planning to do when he got here.

Thomas goes up the steps and enters right in. This strikes Brian as odd. Then he watches as Thomas moves across the living room into the kitchen and straight into Shelly's arms.

"My mom's awake!" Thomas says to her.

"She is?"

"Yea, that's why I can't stay long. I want to spend as much time with her as possible," Thomas says. "I've been told this won't last long."

"Oh, I completely understand," she says as she gives him another huge hug.

"I also wanted to go over some of the things I've been learning about the prison to see if you can add anything."

"Sure," she says as she steps back. "Fire away."

"Did you know a Jennifer Irving? She was an inmate there around the time you volunteered."

"Actually, I do, or I should say more about her than I actually knew her."

"What did you know?"

Shelly leans back against the kitchen counter and thinks. He likes how she shifts her hips so she stands slightly askew. It's sexy, he thinks.

"Not much, really. She was quiet. I think she had been terribly abused through life. I tried communicating with her a couple of times but I was just forcing it and decided to leave her alone. She seemed to relate more to men than women anyway."

"Are you aware she was murdered?"

Shelly shakes her head; this is news to her.

"No. When?"

"About a month or so before your husband quit."

A knowing look comes over Shelly's face. Thomas notices.

"What," he asks.

"That was also the time when Teddy didn't want me to come to the prison anymore. Now I know why," she says.

"He never told you about Jennifer getting killed?"

"Not a word, but that's to be expected. News of what goes on in there never really gets beyond the old stone walls. He should have shared his pain. It might have made him feel better. How'd she die?"

"A woman mutilated her by cutting her up into pieces."

"Oh, God!" Shelly exclaims.

Thomas rubs his face. It's been a long day.

"To top things off, a priest from the cathedral next door to headquarters was found dead earlier today."

"St. Joseph's Old Cathedral?" Shelly says intriguingly.

"Mean something to you?"

Shelly struggles to remember.

"There was someone from the cathedral who helped out at the prison back when Jennifer was killed. He was a volunteer."

"Do you remember his name?" Thomas asks.

Shelly thinks harder.

"Umm...Bob, Bart, something like that."

The connections Thomas is making in his head are growing stronger.

"Brian, maybe?"

"Brian, yes, definitely."

"Do you remember his last name?"

"No, we referred to him as Brother Brian. He was entering the priesthood and lived at the cathedral."

A light bulb goes off in Shelly's head.

"Now that I think of it," she says, "Brian was adamant that Jennifer was in danger from some woman on the ward. I guess he was right."

The connections are too tempting to pass up. He pulls out his phone and calls Brian.

Brian crouches down in the bushes as he watches Thomas and Shelly through the side window. The sight of them happily together unnerves him even more than he already was after killing Father Isaiah. The whole thing makes his heart sink. He doesn't know what to do now.

Everything's falling apart, he thinks. If he kills Shelly, will it make Thomas fall back into despair? If that happens, then who will he save in order to save himself?

All of a sudden, his phone starts ringing. He quickly pulls it out of his pocket and hits the silent button. He peers back in the window; it appears nobody heard the phone from inside the house.

Brian lets out a sigh of relief.

As he relaxes a little, he hears footsteps on the porch of the house next door behind him.

"What are you doing?" the nosy next-door neighbor demands loudly as she looks at Brian hiding in the bushes. Brian jumps up and covers his face with the hood of his coat. He runs from his hiding spot and takes off down the street, leaving clear footprints as he darts across the front lawn.

"Hey, where are you going?" the neighbor screams.

Her yelling captures the attention of Thomas and Shelly inside the house. Thomas looks out the window in time to see the backside of Brian disappear around the corner. He then goes out front. Shelly follows him.

"There was a man hiding and watching you guys from the bushes over here," the neighbor says.

Thomas comes down off the porch and checks out the bushes. He's very careful not to disturb the shoe prints on the front lawn as he takes out his smartphone. He clicks on the flashlight app and inspects the prints. A chill runs down his spine as he recognizes a familiar wear pattern in the snow.

He gets back on his phone and dials up Kayla.

"Kayla, Thomas, can you come over to Shelly's house right away? Bring a crime scene unit with you," he says over the phone.

"What's going on?" she asks.

"We've had a visitor at Shelly's, and I need someone here to oversee the collection of evidence. That's you."

"Is she okay?" Kayla asks.

"She's fine."

"Where are you going to be?"

"I'm gonna follow up on a hunch," he says as he clicks off the phone. He turns to Shelly.

"For now, can you stay at your neighbor's house?" he asks her.

Shelly looks at her neighbor; she shakes her head yes.

"I'll be in touch, but just stay there, for now, okay?" Thomas adds.

"Yea, sure," Shelly responds.

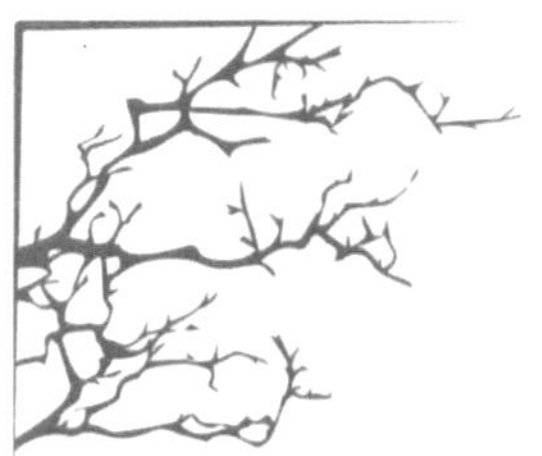

Chapter 46

Thomas makes his way back to the cathedral. The crime scene unit has done all of its work and left. All is quiet; except for the echo of his footsteps as he walks down the main aisle under the high-pitched ceiling toward the altar.

He crosses the altar and makes his way to the door to the rectory. He tries the handle, but it's still locked. The urge to just bust the door open overwhelms him, but he knows if he does that, anything he'd find would probably be worthless in court. And even though it appears there was a crime in the cathedral, he still needs a warrant to get into the private living area of the priests.

Going back out, Thomas makes his way back around the cathedral to the outside door of the rectory. He rings the bell and knocks on the door. Nothing.

Then he feels his phone vibrating in his pocket. He pulls it out and notices it's Brian calling. He answers it.

"Shea, here."

Brian has stationed himself inside the rectory by a second-floor window that is partially blocked from view by the long hanging branches of a pine tree on the side lawn. He watches Thomas' every move.

"I think we should meet," Brian says over the phone.

"I think you're right," Thomas responds. "When and where?"

"Why don't we meet at the concrete grain elevator by Gallagher's Pier in about twenty minutes."

"Interesting choice. Any special reason?" Thomas asks.

"Seems like the place to be."

Thomas hangs up. He then calls Shelly to tell her what's going on.

Brian quickly leaves the second floor and runs out of the backdoor of the rectory to a small parking lot on the other side of the cathedral. He quickly jumps into the Subaru Outback and takes off for the five-minute drive to the abandoned grain elevator on the water's edge.

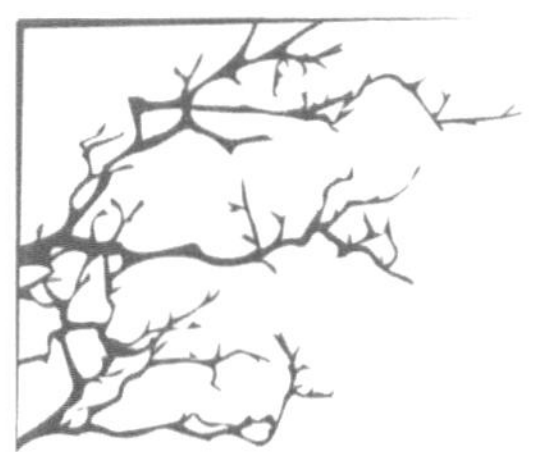

Chapter 47

Thomas drives toward the concrete monolithic structure after entering the driveway to Gallagher's Beach. His headlights shine on the double doors leading inside the abandoned grain elevator. The Subaru Outback Brian drove is parked in front. He pulls up next to where Brian parked and stops. Slowly, he exits the vehicle and surveys his surroundings before walking over to the Subaru to look at the shoe prints in the snow by the driver's door. Disappointment fills his face. His hunch was right.

Looking around, he sees a fresh set of shoe prints going around to the backside of the grain elevator. Thomas decides to go the opposite way around instead of following the trail. He wants to try his best to sneak up on Brian just in case things don't go well.

Thomas carefully walks along a strip of land between the side of the grain elevator and open water as he heads out toward the end of the point. Shadows from trees and bushes on the strip of land dance along the gray walls of the elevator as the winds suddenly begin to howl.

Brian stands at the edge of the point. He's looking out at the ice and water and dark skies rolling over Lake Erie. His coat bottoms flap against the wind. Thomas comes around the corner and hesitates. He looks around to make sure he and Brian are the only ones around in the shadow of the grain elevator.

Slowly Brian turns around and looks at Thomas.

They stare at each other, both motionless.

Thomas cautiously walks toward Brian.

"Hello, Thomas."

"Brian."

The winds whirl around them as they stand almost face to face.

"Is something wrong?" Brian asks almost innocently, but not quite.

Thomas sadly looks at him.

"I just want to know why?"

"Finally pieced it together?"

"I think so."

"I knew you would."

"Again, why?"

Brian gets defiant.

"They were supposed to take care of her," he says. "She was weak and vulnerable, and they all promised me that she would be okay, but she wasn't okay."

"It wasn't their fault."

A rage starts to build in Brian.

"Yes, it was," he says as his voice rises. "They allowed that crazy woman to walk freely around the ward; knowing full well she was completely unstable. Her history was full of unprovoked violence toward others. I begged them to isolate Jennifer to keep her safe from her. I saw how that evil woman was eyeing her up; something was bound to happen."

"How do I fit into all of this?"

The question settles Brian a little. and he smiles.

"Remember when we first met? I told you that sometimes we do things that unsettle our souls, and then we need to find redemption to make it better? Killing those people has unsettled me, but then when I found you, I knew I found my path to redemption. Helping make your soul right hopefully will help save mine."

Thomas' eyes narrow; he doesn't get the logic.

"When you kill innocent people, there's no saving your soul."

"Maybe. But I do have a present for you."

"What's that?"

"I decided not to visit Shelly again. She was going to be my last, but when I saw you together tonight. I saw how she made you smile. That was the only time I've seen you smile," Brian says as his voice turns serious. "You deserve to smile, Thomas."

Brian turns away and removes a syringe from his pocket. He unsheathes it.

Kayla appears alongside the elevator and sees Brian removing the syringe from its case.

"Drop it!" she shouts.

Both Brian and Thomas are startled as Kayla emerges from the darkness with her gun drawn; she's points it at Brian.

Kayla moves in close.

"I said drop it!" she yells again.

Thomas pulls his gun out and points it at Brian.

"What do you got there?" he asks.

Brian turns back to face Thomas.

"You got it wrong; this isn't for you. It's for me," he says as he stares deeply into Thomas' eyes.

Brian suddenly plunges the needle into his neck and drains the syringe before Thomas can move.

Then Brian staggers back to the edge of the point and jumps backward off it. He breaks through the ice and quickly submerges underneath the glassy surface.

Thomas quickly takes off his coat and steps to the edge to dive in.

Kayla grabs him from behind and pulls him back.

"You can't go in," she says.

"Why not?"

"There's no way to get back out. You'll die."

Thomas looks around for a spot to get back out of the water. Thick ice, too thick to break through, surrounds the only metal ladder built into the point's side about 50 yards away. He knows she's right.

Thomas and Kayla step to the edge together and peer over the side. Brian floats motionless face up just under the ice; his eyes staring blankly up at them.

Kayla puts Thomas' coat over his shoulders.

"C'mon, let's call it in and get out of the cold," she says softly.

"Yea."

The End

THE FOLLOWING DAYS were whirlwinds one for Thomas. Shelly came to meet his mom and spent time joking and laughing while they got to know each other a little. They even were able to play a couple of hands of Pinochle. His mom's favorite card game.

The few days they had were great, but it was also quick. Before long, Thomas could see the dull glaze returning to her eyes. He watched as she gently fell back asleep before he settled into the faux leather beige chair to wait out the night. Shelly joins him in his wait. Before long, they also fall asleep as the evening turns to night.

After the bewitching hour passes and before the rise of dawn, Thomas wakes to the soft murmurings of his mom calling out for him. He moves to the side of his mother's bed. She looks up at him, unable to speak clearly, but her eyes say it all.

Her love for her son is immense.

She looks at Shelly asleep in the chair that was brought in for the night. Thomas follows her eyes and also looks at Shelly. Then he looks back at his mother. She has a big smile, and she nods. She struggles as best she can to say her final words.

"I think you're going to be okay now."

She takes a big inhale and then slowly releases it. The heart monitor alarms go off the second her heart stops beating. Thomas bends his head and closes his eyes. When he opens them, Shelly is by his side; holding onto him tightly as they get ready to face a new day together.

Don't miss out!

Visit the website below and you can sign up to receive emails whenever Griffith D Pritchard publishes a new book. There's no charge and no obligation.

https://books2read.com/r/B-A-PONR-LOCVB